Gorgeous George
And the Zigzag Zit-faced Zombies

By
Stuart Reid

Illustrations and Cover
By John Pender

Gorgeous Garage Publishing Ltd
Falkirk, Scotland

Cover design and illustrations by John Pender
Cover and illustrations copyright © Gorgeous Garage Publishing Ltd

Photographs used by kind permission
of Jess Reid and John Pender

Fourth Edition
This edition published in the UK by
Gorgeous Garage Publishing Ltd
ISBN 978-1-910614-04-4

www.stuart-reid.com

DEDICATION

Thanks to my mum and dad for giving
me the love of books.

And for every school, library and book festival
I've ever been invited to perform at...
1,000 and counting!

Reading Rocks!

*For my wife Angela and my little boy Lucas.
Who's love, encouragement and unrelenting
patience means the absolute world me.*

*Thank you for letting daddy
live out his drawing dream!*

*Love always,
John xXx*

iv

CONTENTS

Prologue - Grandpa Jock's Full Stop

You! Yeah you, reading this book. Put it down right now. That's it, close the pages and pop it back onto the book shelf. Don't even think about reading it again!!

You're still reading, aren't ye?

What did I just tell you? Stop blooming reading! It's too dangerous. The secrets in this book have caused way too much trouble for me and George already and don't think I'm coming to rescue your butt if you're abducted by zombies. Once is enough for me. Er...zombies, no. I meant to say 'zebras', yeah, if you're abducted by zebras.

Still reading? You're a brave wee soul, aren't ye? Either that, or just plain stupid.

Well, don't say I didn't warn ye.

Anyway, I knew you'd be difficult aboot this. That's why I don't care if you try to read this book or not. Ye see, the government have secretly implanted an amnesia chip into all the full stops on every page. Yeah, like that one. There's another. And another...

And another three... Right, stop, this could go on for ages so just take my word for it, alright! Every full stop contains a memory erasing laser that wipes your mind from the minute you start reading to the second you stop. Zapped! Just gone.

As soon as you finish reading and close the page, your memory will be automatically scrubbed and you'll remember nothing of this story. But no one would ever believe you if you did.

Please be careful though. If you're reading this on the toilet, remember to wipe your bum afterwards. I've heard of some nasty accidents with the whole reading-a-book-whilst-doing-a-poo scenario. Urgh, messy!

Oh, and if you're reading this on an E-Book, then the

amnesia effect is doubled. You might forget that you've already put the cat out. You might forget that you've already been to the toilet and try to go again.

Then there's what scientists are now calling the Kindle Reaction Auto-brushing Process, or KRAP for short. It's a tricky one so watch out for the effects of this behavioural loop.

You go to bed and read this book. You close the book to go to sleep, but you forget that you've already brushed your teeth so you get up, brush your teeth and come back to bed. Then you start to read this book again and whole cycle begins over.

Some people have almost worn their teeth away overnight becoming trapped in this vicious circle. So again, you have been warned.

Even John the illustrator had to keep the book open for an entire month so he wouldn't forget to draw the pictures for the publisher.

And you can STOP opening and closing this book to see if the memory removal chip is actually working. I know you're doing it, I'm watching you right now. I can see you through the Coma Cameras that are installed in various other pieces of punctuation around the page.

And for goodness sake, stop picking your nose!

However, if for some reason these amnesia chips are faulty and you can remember what you've read, please follow these two wee rules.

Don't take the book back to the shop and say it's broken.

Every bookstore guy and girl in the whole country has read this book, on their tea-breaks usually, (for free!) but of course they can't remember it. So the guy in the book store will have forgotten what you're talking about and may throw you out of the shop.

And DON'T tell anybody what happens! Especially not my grandson George. He can't remember anything about it and thinks it was a plain old boring week after the summer holidays. George must never find out about this – it would freak him out too much.

Honestly, it's for your own good. You're safer not knowing. And I promised the government that I wouldn't say anything about that zombie epidemic we had recently.

Oops! I mean zebras. Ach, too late. Right, last chance....

Stop reading now!

Chapter 1 – Drum Roll

It was the dead of night.

The world was still and lifeless.

A thick fog had rolled in from the coast and was wrapping the countryside in a smothering blanket of mist. This murky gloom hung low across the ground, swirling and flowing around everything it touched.

Sharp, jagged branches reached out unseen from hedgerows and trees to scratch and claw at any unsuspecting passers-by who were foolish enough to venture out on a night as obscure as this.

In the sky above, the clouds blocked out any light from the moon and the stars. The grey fog a shade lighter than black; a sombre deception that gave no hint to the depth of darkness beyond.

It was as if Death itself had lain down to sleep in the shadowy landscape; silent, stagnant and alone in a grim reaper's graveyard.

Yet, occasionally when a breath of air would part the mists, off in the distance a faint orange glow could be seen as if hovering in the sky; the street lights from a small town.

And on the hillside road leading around this isolated, urban sprawl two vehicles were driving faster than the foggy darkness should have allowed.

Leading the race was a jet black, four-wheel drive cruiser; fast and imposing, with dusky windows, being driven hard with its headlights off. Switching the lights on would've meant a blinding reflection from the fog and the man behind the wheel was well trained to drive in the dark. Even from within his yellow rubber suit and helmet.

Behind the cruiser was a large, flat bed truck, drab olive green in colour and trying desperately to keep up with the speeding car. The truck was old and rickety, and laden with rusting barrels of liquid that slopped from side to side as the truck driver threw the vehicle viciously around every bend.

The truck bounced and jolted on the road, gravel flying up with every missed corner. This driver too wore a yellow rubber suit, with a clear glass visor and an air-hose from the back of his helmet leading to a small tank sitting on the passenger seat.

They were in a hurry.

In fact, they were in so much of a rush to leave the chemical plant one technician had failed to strap down the barrels at the back end of the truck properly. The constant motion as they rolled around every junction began to loosen and slacken off the buckle that was meant to be holding the containers in place.

It was inevitable then, whilst the truck careered around another savagely sharp bend, that one of the barrels would break free from the strapping, topple over the flimsy guardrail and crash down the hill. The drum rolled and rolled, bouncing and bumping over rocks and bushes until it finally came to rest, still sealed, at the edge of Little Lake Pump.

Fog drifted in off the lake and surrounded the barrel, all momentum almost lost in the impact. The water lapped against the metal as the drum finally ceased rocking and came to complete rest. There was a brief pause, a misleading lull in activity before the three clips on the drum's lid pinged off in quick succession.

Poing! Poing! Poing!

The lid splashed down into the water and a bright, green liquid oozed out of the barrel. Steam evaporated from the fluid as soon as it made contact with the water.

The chemical burned into every piece of vegetation that it

touched around the perimeter of the lake; grass and flowers withering as the acidic secretion leaked out. Wisps of smoke drifted into the air from the smouldering embers.

Soon, the lake began to glow with a lime phosphorous vapour, which puffed up into the air all across the surface and eventually the entire body of water was boiling and bubbling as plant life on the lake bed was incinerated by the toxins.

This vapour hung heavy in the atmosphere, almost sparkling green amongst the grey fog swirling around before the silence and stillness returned to the countryside. The mist smothered the noise once more as the tomb-like tranquillity settled back into the darkness.

Chapter 2 – Grandpa Jock Butts In

So you're still reading this, then? Were ye no' listening?

Or maybe you've already read it and then forgotten about it so you're reading this bit again.

Well, if you're going to persist I might as well give ye a bit of background information. Knowledge is power, as they say. (But try getting knowledge to work in a power cut, it's useless. Candles are much better.)

We live in Little Pumpington, in the north east of England. It's a pretty wet and windy place at the best of times but it could be worse. There used to be a dirty, smelly power plant on the hill above the town and on the hour, every hour the three chimneys would blast off huge plumes of dirty black smoke into the air. The place used to really stink.

Then some local nutcase invented a clean, green, environmentally friendly, alternative energy before we threw him (and his wife) in jail for 15,000 years. Trust me, they deserved it! And after that a group of rampaging old age pensioners trashed his power plant and turned it into the largest surround sound cinema in Europe.

And George thinks Little Pumpington is the most boring town in Britain? It has its moments!

George is ten and lives with his mum and dad and occasionally his big sister Henrietta, when she's home from university. I live roond the corner in a quiet, wee cul-de-sac.

I'm George's Grandpa Jock, by the way, but most people call me Mr Jock…… or that mad old duffer…or that mental old heidbanger at the end of the street…….. or the completely barking, gingered haired yet still baldy pensioner who's a liability to himself and everybody else who goes near him! I should know; I've heard them talking aboot me.

So what if I still like going on scooters. Yes, I love playing my bagpipes; even if my neighbours think I'm shoving fireworks up cats' bottoms (please don't try this at home), I just need a bit more practice, that's all (playing the bagpipes that is, not shoving fireworks up cats' butts. That wouldn't be good).

And yes, I may have committed the rest of my life to being irresponsible, never growing up and having as much fun as possible but that shouldn't class me as a nutter. Live life for the now, is my motto. Carpe diem is a posh way to say it. That's Latin for 'seize the day' but I prefer 'squeeze the day' - grabbing as many days as I have left and squashing every bit of entertainment out of each of them.

My grandson George is good fun too. On the outside, he can be a bit serious but we love having a laugh together. Poo, pee and pumps are our usual sources of humour.

He's got a really good friend too. Allison is a very smart, very responsible young lady, which is quite a good thing because without her maturity, George would have been in a spot of bother more than a few times.

But this little problem with the zombies..... As far as we can tell, it all started in the school.

Anyway, sorry for all the interruptions. I'll let ye get back to the story.

Chapter 3 – Crush

Rebuilding Little Pumpington primary school had taken the whole summer. It wasn't difficult to demolish the old school, George's explosion had done most of that last year and now the town had a brand spanking new facility to be proud of.

Most of the money used in the construction of the new school was raised by the council through the sell-off of the school playing fields. These pitches had always been costly to maintain and they were hardly ever used, either because the long grass needed cut or heavy rain had turned the surface into a quagmire. Either way, if the pitch was to be played on by the school football team, the first twenty minutes of every match was spent looking out for the multiple piles of dog poo that would litter the grass.

So, instead of being the largest toilet in the north east of England, a shopping centre was built right on top of the football pitches where dozens of shops were waiting to open for business. The grand opening was scheduled for next week and the shops were setting up, ready for business. It didn't matter that they were selling all the same stuff the shops on Little Pumpington High St sold but under the one roof, safe from the wind and rain.

And instead of that old crumbling shambles of an educational establishment this new school was a wonderful octagonal structure, two storeys tall and complete with eight classrooms, a pre-school crèche and a state-of-the-art kitchen and dining room which doubled, or trebled as an assembly hall with a stage. There was a small garden in the centre of the classrooms and there was even a weather station on the roof.

The playground was spacious and colourful with a soft play park for the nursery pupils and there was a planting area with a greenhouse made out of 2 litre plastic juice bottles. Off in the corner, near the new shopping centre, was a modern multi-use games area called a MUGA; an all-weather soft surface with painted blue and red railings all the way round to keep the ball in play and goals at either end painted white. The MUGA entrance was on the halfway line but children usually enjoyed jumping through the crawl space at the side of each goalpost.

But this marvellous new building wasn't the reason George had brushed his hair today. It wasn't why he'd given his teeth an extra hard brush this morning. His mum had asked him why he was using his dad's deodorant; this was all rather odd behaviour.

George had even asked his friend Allison to check up his nostrils to make sure he didn't have any loose bogies hanging around. Allison suspected there was something going on.

Then she was sure of it, when George was first to put his hand up to answer every question in their new classroom every day this week.

This year Miss Davenport was their teacher, fresh from teacher training college, bubbling with energy and enthusiasm, with a wide, radiant smile that showed off her perfect white teeth. Her brown, shoulder length hair was pulled back in a loose ponytail and her dark eyes sparkled with wisdom.

'You fancy her!' whispered Allison.

George didn't reply. He was staring straight ahead, his jaw slack and his head propped up on his elbow. There was a dreamy, watery look in his eyes.

'See! You really fancy her,' said Allison again, nudging George with her elbow.

'Eh? What?' George sat up from his trance...
'Er, no I don't.'

12

'Yeah you do,' giggled Allison. 'You've sat there like a zombie since we came back from summer holidays. You can't take your eyes off her.'

'It just makes a nice change from that old dragon Mrs Watt, that's all.' But George's protests fell on deaf ears.

'Boys and girls, I know we were all working hard yesterday on your eco-projects about sustainability,' sang Miss Davenport (well, at least the words sang in George's ears). 'Now today we need three volunteers to present our work to.....'

Before she could finish her sentence George's hand shot straight up in the air.

'Creep!' whispered a quiet voice sitting behind George. George turned and saw it was Crayon Kenny, the boy known to every doctor in Little Pumpington. Kenny pretended to stick two fingers down his throat and gagged.

'Thank you George,' smiled Miss Davenport, 'but you don't even know what we're going to do yet.'

'I don't mind, Miss Davenport,' beamed George, running to the front of the class.

'Bleugh' choked Kenny quietly, unable to take any more of George's sugary sweetness.

'Well, we'll be presenting our work to Mrs Macpherson's infants' class, who are learning about the environment.'

George's heart sank. He'd been eager to impress Miss Davenport but didn't realise he'd be going to see Mrs Macpherson's class. Mrs Macpherson was George's first teacher at Little Pumpington primary school and she'd made his life a misery with her constant criticism and continual desire to force George to 'aspire to something nobler.' Whatever that meant. George always thought she was trying to brainwash him.

And she certainly didn't appreciate George's imagination or freedom of thought.

13

'I think we need a girl now,' Miss Davenport nodded. 'Perhaps to start off the presentation. A strong vocal leader.'

At this Allison perked up her ears. She enjoyed reading in class and any opportunity to talk in front of an audience appealed to her. She thrust her hand into the air.

'Excellent Allison, thank you,' gushed their teacher. Allison stepped out from behind her desk and went to stand beside George.

'Now we just need one more presenter to make up the group?' asked Miss Davenport, appealing to the class. There were no volunteers. Every head dropped and no one wanted to make eye contact.

'But we could manage ourselves, Miss,' simpered George.

'Bleeeeeeuuuuggghh!' gagged Kenny, now no longer able to tolerate George's over-the-top politeness.

'And we've found our last volunteer,' said Miss Davenport with her eyes narrowing in on Kenny. 'Haven't we, Mr Roberts?'

Kenny sighed. He didn't mean to say it so loud but George was sticking his head so far up the teacher's butt he could see what she had for breakfast. And now Kenny was dragging himself out from behind his desk to join George and Allison at the front of the class.

George, however, was unimpressed. He could not believe Miss Davenport had chosen one of the most unpredictably idiotic boys he'd ever met as his partner for the presentation.

On a good day Kenny Roberts could be described as slightly eccentric. On other days Kenny could be certified as stark raving bonkers. Kenny was famous, both in school and all around Little Pumpington for his unusual hobby of sticking crayons, buttons, brussel sprouts, bananas, small toy cars and pretty much anything else up his nose and sometimes into other orifices.

Most of the nurses and doctors at Little Pumpington General Hospital were on first name terms with his parents and it was rumoured they had a special pair of forceps with Kenny's name on them.

'I wonder if they ever managed to find all the marbles that were stuck up his bottom?' whispered George.

'Shhhh!' hushed Allison, as Kenny approached. Allison didn't think this was funny but clearly she'd heard about 'the bag of marbles incident'. Allegedly, Kenny was still discussing his 'achievement' with the Guinness Book of Records.

'Hi George, hey Allison,' grunted Kenny as he joined them in the line.

'Hey Kenny, what's up?' smirked George. Allison shot him a vicious look.

'Nothing yet,' replied Kenny with a wink, 'but the night is young. George sniggered.

'Don't let him near those paper clips, George,' whispered Allison. Kenny smiled and wiggled his eyebrows.

'What are we meant to be doing here again?' said Kenny, staring at his feet as Miss Davenport was explaining what the class would be doing in her absence. She had lined up a written exercise, a reading assignment and a short quiz of the chapter. Mr Winchester the new Head teacher would be dropping in to check on them now and again.

'Weren't you listening yesterday?' asked Allison.

'No, not really,' replied Crayon Kenny. 'I had er…. misplaced my rubber at the time. You know, the tiny little one from the end of a pencil.' George sniggered again.

'I got it back though. Still works too. Once I dried it off a bit.' Kenny was talking incessantly in a low, hushed tone. 'I've never presented before. What do you do, just make it up on the spot?'

'Here, read these.' And George handed Kenny a small pile of postcard with a few words and phrases written on them. 'These are prompter cards to fit in with our presentation.'

'We wrote a presentation yesterday??' Kenny really had been distracted.

'Yes, and we've to present it to the junior class this morning. I wrote out these prompts last night.'

Kenny nudged Allison. 'I told you he was a teacher's pet.'

'Not usually,' replied Allison. 'He's just got a thing for the new teacher.'

'Yeah,' laughed Kenny. 'I noticed. But thanks anyway.'

Kenny held on tightly to the postcards and looked a little relieved. His bravado was showing cracks now the reality of speaking to an entire class was imminent. Not just any class. The infants!

'You said the junior class, didn't you?' Things were becoming clearer to Kenny now. 'Those little freaks are absolutely mental.'

'You'll be fine, dude,' said George, trying to reassure him but it wasn't really working.

'My little brother's in that class. They are nutters,' Kenny went on. 'The laws of good manners and common decency just don't apply to them. They say what they want, when they want. Honesty to the point of brutality.'

'Honesty's not a bad thing.' And George stared across at Miss Davenport again dewy eyed.

'You're a proper little Romeo today, aren't you,' smirked Allison.

'They can see through phonies.' Kenny was now rapping the cards against his leg. 'And they can sense fear. I've heard they rip visitors to shreds.'

'Just chill, man.' But it was too late. Their time had come.

'Alright, marvellous,' sang Miss Davenport as she turned to the students standing at the front of the classroom. 'And I think you three make a wonderful team. You'll do the class proud.'

One or two of the other girls in the class had looked a little disappointed not to be picked but the rest of them didn't seem too bothered. Certainly all the other boys looked rather relieved George and Kenny had been chosen and it would appear that those years of strict, disciplinary tutoring from the ancient Mrs Watt and the other teachers like her had sucked the enthusiasm from the children and educated them to within an inch of their lives.

George had always thought teachers had a hard job. Long ago they could just beat children with canes and belts and ruled their classrooms by fear. Nowadays, not only did they have mould their teaching methods around Human Rights but they were up against TVs and DVDs and games consoles and computers and instant gratification of an online world. Teachers now had to inspire their pupils to make learning fun; they needed to engage and involve children to want to explore subjects or test theories or read more.

These older teachers had been set in their ways for decades and changing their style was a terrifying thought. Those that couldn't adapt usually became bitter, old dinosaurs desperately clinging onto the only power and control they knew and retirement couldn't come quickly enough for them, or the next generation of nursery pupils waiting to step up into primary school.

Miss Davenport had only been a proper teacher for three days and her natural style was to encourage and motivate and develop young minds. It was going to take the young woman longer than that to break through the malaise that had formed over years of bad teaching. The children had been suffocated but George had enough motivation for the whole class.

He practically bounced along the corridor beside Miss Davenport with Allison behind him and Kenny dragging along at the back. Kenny and Allison kept exchanging glances as George talked constantly.

'Do you want me to start the presentation, Miss Davenport?'

'Or maybe Allison can start and I'll flip the pages over for her on the laptop. I've given Kenny his words to read and I'll finish off. If that's okay with you, Miss Davenport? I've written out the presentation on these cards, so we don't forget them. Will you be staying to watch, Miss?'

'He's unbelievable,' whispered Kenny. 'He's absolutely infatuated with her.'

'It's a schoolboy crush thing, Kenny. He'll grow out of it.'

Then Allison nudged him to show off a cheeky impersonation of George almost skipping along beside his new teacher. Kenny laughed and felt better.

As they reached the top of the stairs Mr Winchester was bursting through the double doors.

Mr Winchester was the new Head teacher at Little Pumpington Primary. The last Head had retired after the scandal involving his principal teacher, his old janitor and the secret stash of false teeth in his school. Mr Winchester was actually a secondary school teacher who wanted to fast-track his career by taking up a senior position in a primary school.

He was tall and slim, with short dark hair and a goatee beard. He was carrying an armful of papers and didn't even acknowledge the group as they approached. Instead Mr Winchester glanced at them and took off in the opposite direction.

'Mr Winchester? Mr Winchester, excuse me one second,' cried Miss Davenport politely.

'Don't stop me now!' he yelled back. 'I'm not having a good time this morning.'

'You are remembering to check on my class a couple times in the next forty-five minutes, aren't you?'

'Yes, yes, check on small children, yes!' and he didn't wait for a reply, walking as fast as possible without seeming like he was running away.

'Is it true, Miss, Mr Winchester has never worked in a primary school before?' asked Allison curiously.

'No, I don't think so,' replied Miss Davenport, 'but he is very ambitious so he should do a very good job.'

'I don't think he likes little kids,' said Kenny. 'He always runs passed us in the corridor. He never speaks.'

'My dad says that people who rush around carrying files and paperwork are just trying to look busy,' said George carefully, 'but they don't actually do anything. And nobody stops them.'

'I'm sure Mr Winchester is a very busy man, George,' answered Miss Davenport, wanting to give the most appropriate reply but George was sure she had thoughts of her own.

'Well, my dad says that ambition shouldn't be mistaken for the ability to do a good job,' said Allison. 'Ambitious people are just good at making themselves look very efficient so they get promoted.'

'I hope Mr Winchester will be with us for quite some time,' Miss Davenport squirmed, not quite sure if she should be continuing this conversation and she hurried down the stairs.

They all looked at each other. George and Kenny whispered 'Chancer!' at exactly the same moment before they ran to catch up.

Chapter 4 – Presenting...

Eventually they'd all walked downstairs and around the corridor to reach the infants classroom at the far end of the school, beyond the assembly/dining hall and kitchen on one side and the gymnasium on the other. As soon as Miss Davenport opened the thick fire doors to the corridor on the ground floor they were hit by a wall of noise. Shouting, shrieking, screaming, singing, drums banging and trumpets tooting.

'Perhaps Mrs Macpherson's not in her classroom,' said Miss Davenport, raising her eyebrows. She opened the door to the classroom and the noise got louder. Small children were running around wildly, paper aeroplanes were whizzing around the classroom, colourful streamers were being flung between desks, paper hankies were being waved furiously and it was a general scene of absolute mayhem and chaos.

Kenny's little brother Johnny waved across as they walked in. Johnny was five and was following in his big brother's footsteps by inserting strange objects into different parts of his anatomy. Johnny had recently discovered he could 'hide' small buttons up his bum and their mum was so horrified by this behaviour she'd immediately bought him three large bars of chocolate as a bribe. Johnny had quickly seen the advantages of this type of negotiation.

Running through the mayhem, Johnny jumped towards Kenny with a final 'thump', landing at his big brother's feet.

'Can I have some candy?' Johnny asked, patting Kenny's pockets.

'No, course not,' said Kenny forcefully. 'You're in class.'

'Then I'll have to eat my bogies,' Johnny shouted, as if to try and persuade his big brother to give him sweets. 'If I'm hungry.'

'See if I care, you little weirdo,' replied Kenny, turning to

George and Allison. 'I don't know where he gets it from,' said Kenny with a smile.

'Indoor voices, children please!' announced Miss Davenport, in a crisp, clear and authoritative voice. The children fell silent immediately and began returning quickly to the seats. The paper planes slowly descended to the ground, the streamers softly bobbed onto the desks and the hankies settled gently onto the floor.

As normality returned George could see the teacher's desk in the far corner of the classroom. Slumped across the flat surface with her head buried in the crook of her arm was the head of a greying old woman. Surprised by the sudden silence, she sat bolt upright, hair dishevelled and wild.

'Sorry to disturb you, Mrs Macpherson,' said Miss Davenport softly as she approached the desk 'My pupils are here for their presentation on sustainability to your class.'

'Oh yes, yes, of course,' Mrs Macpherson stammered. 'We were in the middle of free time, just waiting on you coming down really.' Her piggy little eyes looked blood-shot and tired. Then, rather self-consciously, she snatched the brown bottle that was sitting to her right and thrust it into the desk drawer.

'Erm, cough medicine, er…. ' she said, not wishing to make eye-contact with anyone. 'We had a class trip to visit Little Lake Pump yesterday and some of the children are running a fever today. Just a bit of a sniffle really, I'm making sure they're feeling better.'

Miss Davenport leaned in closer and whispered. 'I'm sure you are aware we're not supposed to dispense medicines in class. The school nurse should……'

'Of course I am aware!' snapped the old teacher. 'But I didn't study four years at university to wipe the noses of snotty little five year olds! After forty years of teaching, I'm quite capable of looking after these brats.'

George glanced across at Allison and Kenny and made a bug-eyes face. Kenny laughed. Mrs Macpherson didn't seem capable of looking after herself at times, never mind controlling or inspiring a classroom of excitable youngsters. She might've been in the teaching profession for four decades but George thought she was losing the will and the inclination to even enforce her rule of fear some days.

'These are my pupils who'll be talking to your class today,' and Miss Davenport opened her hand out to present George, Allison and Kenny.

Without looking up, Mrs Macpherson took a paper handkerchief from the sleeve of her grey cardigan, wiped her nose with it, and then tucked it back into position. She finally lifted her head to acknowledge the three older pupils standing behind Miss Davenport.

'Oh my, what a treat we're in for,' sneered Mrs Macpherson. 'The idiot crayon boy and the imbecile Hansen.' She stared at George with disgust. 'And I don't know who you are girl but I doubt if you'll amount to much,'

George glanced at Allison and her face was seething red. Miss Davenport was about to step across to the desk when Mrs Macpherson quickly jumped from her desk and walked around the other side to avoid her.

'Boys and girls!' shrieked Mrs Macpherson. 'We have a special......er.... surprise for you today.' The words seem to stick in the older teacher's throat. Learning wasn't about surprises; it was about beating knowledge into children's heads until it stayed there. 'These three....er... pupils from one of the older classes are here to tell you about the environment or something. Sit up, pay attention and no talking.'

Miss Davenport nodded to George who went over to the laptop at the side of the whiteboard and switched it on. The screen flashed to life and George stuck the little pen drive into the USB port. With a couple of clicks of the mouse he'd found the presentation his class had prepared. He winked over to Allison, who nodded back whilst Miss Davenport took a seat at the front and motioned to Kenny to sit beside her. George sat next to the laptop and started the presentation.

Allison turned to face the class and smiled. 'Good morning everybody. Today I'd like to tell you what it means to be green.' Allison pointed to a picture of the world on the screen.

'Sustainability is about looking after the planet and making things last for a long time- maybe forever. It's not just like cleaning up your bedroom – it's about keeping tidy a great big huge room that belongs to everyone! And if we mess it up, we mess it up for everybody else.'

George clicked on the button and the picture of the Earth changed to three green, linking arrows forming an ever-lasting chain. Allison started talking about recycling rubbish, reusing things that would normally be thrown away and reducing the amount of energy that's used. George had helped write this slide so he knew Allison had about three minutes to expand on these points. He relaxed and sat back in his chair, staring out at the sea of eager young faces staring up at Allison.

Only this sea wasn't blue. This sea of faces was almost green in colour. George stared in amazement. Every one of the little kids looking up at Allison had two trails of green snot dripping down from their noses. They were all absolutely covered in the slime!

Some of them occasionally wiped their sleeves over their faces. This only helped to smear the snot over their jumpers and across the back of their hands. Most of the kids looked like they'd had armies of snails crawling up their arms, leaving long, thin, slimy trails behind them.

Worse than that, some of the pupils would lick their top lip with their tongue, slurping up the gunge and dragging it back down into their mouths. George started to feel a bit queasy as he watched the little snot bandits feast upon the mucus running down from their nostrils.

George tried hard to concentrate on Allison's speech, then on Kenny's part but his eyes were constantly dragged back to the scene of slippery secretion. It was like a car crash; he knew he shouldn't look but it was grossly fascinating. He'd never seen so much snotter in his life.

Some of the youngsters played with it, slurping it back and forth. None of them were disgusted by it and most of them seemed to enjoy it. It was their very own special supply of Play-dough.

Kenny's little brother Johnny was making good his threat to eat his own bogies as he scraped the contents out with his fingernails.

Even as his own section of the presentation started, George had to fight to focus on the words on his cards and on the wall at the back of the room, avoiding all eye contact with the class. He knew if he caught sight of another mucus muncher he'd lose his place and fumble his words.

'….and it's like a big circle; everything goes around. It's about taking care of the planet and its creatures and why we must think about only using what you need rather than what you want. Thank you.' George stopped a little uncertainly and looked across at Miss Davenport, who began clapping enthusiastically. The rest of the class, with the exception of Mrs Macpherson, all joined in with applause.

George felt a little relieved and smiled over to Allison and

Kenny, who joined him in taking a small bow. George then ejected the pen drive and followed Miss Davenport towards the door. Mrs Macpherson walked with her and stopped abruptly as Miss Davenport turned.

'Thank you children, for your excellent listening skills and to Mrs Macpherson too, for allowing Allison, George and Kenny to talk with you this morning.' And she opened the door.

'It's all rubbish, you know,' muttered Mrs Macpherson. 'This global warming and recycling nonsense. It's just a ploy to make money for big businesses.'

'Thank you for your time, Mrs Macpherson,' smiled Miss Davenport. 'I'm sure we'll have to agree to disagree but I think it would be crazy not to teach children about their environment.'

'Crazy? These kids are a bunch of crazies! No good wasters, the lot of them,' spat the old teacher, pushing the class room door closed.

Miss Davenport turned on her heels and marched off down the corridor with her shoulders back and her head high.

'That Macpherson is just like our old teacher, Mrs Watt. Another nutcase,' whispered Kenny.

'Never mind nutcases, 'said Allison in a low voice. 'What about those disgusting little kids? Each and every one of them was picking their noses!'

'And eating it!' added Kenny. It was Allison's turn to look queasy.

'Oh, I know!' yelled George, 'I was trying not to look. Your little brother must've been starving.'

'Yeah, he was having a right good scratch up each nostril and scoffing up the contents; the whole class was! You should see them biting every last morsel from underneath their fingernails.'

'Thank you Kenneth for reminding us of that hideous vision,' Allison declared haughtily. 'But they were filthy,' she said lowering her tone. 'A few kids were trying to hide that fact they were eating their boogers. Discreetly nibbling behind their hands.'

'Most of them didn't care. It was like a three course dinner up there,' added George. 'What about the ones who were drinking their own snot? And the crusty bits.....Eeuugghh!'

'No, no, wait. Did you see the little kid who was digging so far up his nose that it started to bleed,' yakked Kenny. 'No joking, his nose was bleeding faster than he could lick it up. I think he was too scared of that mad old teacher to admit it because he used his shirt to mop up the excess. He was covered.'

'They are a disgusting little bunch,' admitted Allison, with a nod. 'But they were all a little bit too keen.'

'What do you mean?' asked George, with a raised, puzzled eyebrow.

'I just think we need to investigate something a bit further, that's all.'

Chapter 5 – Under the Desks

Just as they were arriving back in their classroom the interval bell began to ring. All their classmates jumped up and filed out towards the stairs. George, Kenny and Allison stepped into the room as Miss Davenport was leaving too.

'We're just going to put away our things,' said Allison helpfully, holding up her notes.

'Yes, good. Thank you,' replied Miss Davenport a little distractedly. 'Well done for this morning. I'm just off to the staffroom to have words with.....er one of the other teachers. You clear away your things and run along outside.'

'Yes, Miss,' answered George.

'Yes, miss. No, miss, three bags full, miss' squeaked Kenny, screwing up his face and rocking his head back and forth. 'Can I carry your briefcase, miss? Can I kiss your shoes, miss?'

George's face was bright red. His ears were the same burning colour as his hair.

'I just think she's a very good teacher, that's all,' said he nonchalantly. 'At least I haven't lost an entire packet of crayons up my nose before.'

Kenny laughed. 'You should try it, mate. Rainbow bogies are brilliant.'

George smiled. Kenny was completely cuckoo but he could be good fun at times.

'Be quiet, you two.' Allison was watching down the corridor through the crack of the door. As Miss Davenport disappeared down the stairs Allison gently closed the door and ran over to the desks. She dropped onto her knees and rolled over onto her back. She was now lying on the classroom floor staring up at the ceiling. George and Kenny just stared at her.

'Tired, are you?'

'Need a bit of a lie down?'

Allison was scrambling backwards, shuffling herself along on her back from desk to desk.

'Come and see this.' Allison could be quite demanding when she was in full flow and her flow was filling up fast. 'Look.'

George and Kenny kneeled down beside her and stared up at where she was pointing. The underside of every desk was covered with a multi-coloured layer of chewing gum jammed into every corner. Pink, white, grey and yellow blobs of gunk were stuck fast onto the patchwork surface.

'Chewing gum,' shrugged George. 'So what? No one wants to get caught chewing gum in class.'

'Look closer.' Allison was now using the tip of her pen to point upwards to the crusted green and yellow shapes in the centre of the desk.

'Is that......dried bogies?' asked George, screwing up his nose. Allison was careful not to touch the crusts, in case they flaked off and dropped down onto her face.

'Uh, they're under every desk.' Kenny was now scrambling on his knees between each row.

'Right. Now let's get back down to the infant class, whilst they're all playing outside.' And Allison jumped to her feet and ran to the door. George and Kenny just stared at each other.

'Bogies?' said Kenny. 'Is she always like this?'

'Don't stop her now,' sighed George. 'She's having a good time!'

George and Kenny had to run hard to catch up with Allison. She was already down the stairs, along the corridor and into the classroom before they reached her. She was down on her hands and knees again, crawling around under the desks.

'What have you found this time?' asked George.

'Nothing' replied Allison.

'Nothing at all?' George dropped to his knees and searched under the desk closest to him.

'I'm not surprised,' said Kenny, standing in the doorway. 'Little kids aren't allowed chewing gum; they choke on it.'

'I'm not looking for chewing gum,' replied Allison, 'It was to see more bogies.'

'Bogies?' gasped George and Kenny together.

'You're as weird as my little brother,' giggled Kenny. 'And he's obsessed with his bogies.'

Yeah,' laughed George. 'You keep sticking stuff up your nose and he's always pulling stuff out.'

'That's my point,' snapped Allison seriously. 'Two or three kids in every class will be fixated with picking their noses. Maybe four, or five, let's say as many as ten. But the whole class? Every one of them, obsessed with their snots. It's not normal.'

'Mrs Macpherson did say they'd been out on a field trip yesterday and had caught colds,' suggested George. 'Maybe that's why they were all sniffing and sneezing.'

'But the summer holidays have just finished, George. It's still warm outside,' argued Allison. 'There's no way they'd all catch colds. And look, there isn't a single bogie under any of these desks.'

George stood and thought for a second. 'You may have a point actually,' he admitted. 'Not every kid would want to eat their own bogies. If they've been picking their nose, most of them would wipe their boogers under the desk; we saw that in our class.....'

'But here......' gasped Allison. 'There's nothing....It's as if they've been........'

THUMP!

The noise came from the back of the classroom. George, Allison and Kenny all turned.

'Hallo?' shouted George.

'Is there somebody there?' asked Kenny, edging around the last row of desks. George and Allison crept behind him.

There, under one of the desks at the edge of the classroom, was a small girl in a blue checked dress and blonde pigtails. She was kneeling upwards with her face pressed against the underside of the desk.

'Is she......' stammered Allison. 'Is she...... licking the desk?'

'Aw, man,' groaned George, 'she's eating the crusty bogies from underneath the desks. She's on her last one; she's licked them all clean.'

'Gross!' shrieked Allison and the little girl looked up at her with a ravenous glint in her eye. At first it was a protective 'keep away' growl, as the small child held onto her desk tightly. With a hungry realisation that a fresh feast was close at hand, the girl began to stand up slowly. Drool hung down from the side of her face and her heavy eyes, with the dark bags beneath, looked sluggish and puffy.

'Bogggggiiees,' she muttered in a long drawn out drawl.

'Did she just say "Bogies"?' asked George with a smile.

'Boh,' she began again. 'Bogggggiiiieeeesssssss!'

'That would be a 'yes', George,' laughed Kenny. 'The tiny snot licker wants to eat your bogies, Allison.'

'Urgh, keep the little monster away from me,' said Allison as she recoiled back towards the door.

'Bogggggggggggggiiiiiiiiiiiiieeeeeeeeeeesssssssss!!' growled the girl with a more determined grimace. She staggered to her feet and began swaying towards the other three. There were two green streams of snot flowing freely from her nostrils and she licked it up eagerly, her tongue flicking out across her top lip like a serpents'.

'Let's go,' urged Allison. 'I really don't want that disgusting child touching me.' And she turned and opened the door quickly. Kenny and George were still giggling when they closed the classroom door behind them. The corridor was empty and the distant sound of squeals and shrieks echoed from the playground.

They turned left heading passed the kitchen and the assembly hall toward the side exit. As they rounded the last corner they all stopped. A small boy had just entered the door from the playground and was staggering towards them.

'Look, here comes another one of the little nutters,' laughed Kenny.

'He's a bit unsteady on his feet, don't you think?' replied Allison. 'He's bouncing off the walls.'

'Mrs Macpherson's probably given him too much cough medicine,' sniggered George as he watched the kid slowly zigzag along the corridor, swaying from side to side. As he got closer the two green trails of snot flowing from his nose became obvious and Allison turned her head and hid her eyes from the mess.

'Uh, that's vile,' said Allison, using her hand to shield her eyes from the slime.

'He's coming for you, Allison!' George was now pretending to stagger along like Frankenstein's monster. 'He's going to get you!'

'George, stop being a child,' yelled Allison.

'He's coming to get you, Allison!' George went on.

'George, you're acting like an idiot.' Allison was backing away and trying to maintain her maturity but her legs desperately wanted to run in the other direction. The little kid was closer than ever, still staggering and bouncing off the walls but relentlessly coming towards them.

The boy's eyes looked dull and lifeless and his mouth hung open to catch the mucus that dripped down.

His skin was pale and there were two heavy dark bags under his eyes. His face was covered in yellow pus-filled spots like an acne-ridden teenager. He looked ill.

Then, without warning and with a speed that belied his drugged up state the small boy jumped at Allison, attacking her and dragging her to the ground. Allison screamed but her voice was soon muffled as the boy's small fingers began to claw furiously at her face.

'George, help! He's picking my nose!' Allison yelled as George and Kenny grabbed the boy's arms and tried to pull him away. Pinned back, the boy dipped his head forward and snatched at her nose with his mouth. He didn't bite, just wrapped his lips around Allison's nostrils and started slurping wildly.

'He's sucking out my nose, George! Get him off! Get him off!' Allison screamed.

With an enormous tug George and Kenny yanked the little kid off her and threw him across the floor. He lay motionless against a coat rack and a pile of school bags.

'What's happening to them?' shouted George. 'The little dudes are going mad. They're infected or something.'

'I think you're right, George' replied Kenny running off around the corner. 'But I've got to check on my little brother.' And with that Kenny disappeared through the next set of fire doors towards the infant's playground. Allison took a few steps after him and stopped.

'I wonder what's happening to them,' asked George. 'I mean, they are daft but they're not usually violent. It's like the infants have......'

The words caught in George's throat. The small boy had leapt onto George's back and was scratching at his nose with nasty little fingernails. With each potential mouthful the boy nibbled on his fingers hoping to taste some of George's bogies.

Allison could think of nothing else to do than charge straight at the struggling pair. She barged into them, knocking both of them to the ground; George banged his head against the floor whilst the angry kid was able to land softy amongst the pile of school bags again. He slowly dragged himself back onto his feet again and stared at Allison with an insatiable craving.

Without a second thought Allison turned on her heels and ran for the exit door at the end of the corridor. She pushed it open wide, ran into the empty playground and stopped. The yard was completely empty. There wasn't a single child anywhere to be seen. Dirty white paper hankies and snotty tissues blew silently across the playground in the pale light. The sun was eerily low in the sky and was casting long dark shadows across the ground.

Where was everyone?

Chapter 6 - Crash

'Bogggggiiieeeeeeeeeeeeeeees'

The growling behind her was getting louder and Allison turned to see the spotty yet bogie-hungry pupil standing by the doorway on the school. Allison ran across the empty playground towards the teachers' car park and leapt over the low fence. The heel of her shoe snagged on the wire and she desperately kicked it off as the pale-faced pupil stumbled towards her.

'Bogggggiiieeeeeeeeeeeeeeees'

Hobbling now, she slipped and slid between the cars, frantically trying every door handle on every car, hoping and praying that one would eventually give her sanctuary. The bogie-boy had crossed the playground and was now shambling over the fence. Between sneezes he staggered from car to car, closing in on Allison.

Sobbing a little, Allison pulled at the heel of her remaining shoe and threw it at the growling youngster. It hit him on the head but that didn't seem to have any effect; the snarling zombie with dark shadows under its eyes staggered onwards, unrelenting, unstoppable.

Eventually Allison felt a click of a lock and she pulled open the car door. One of the teachers had been in a rush that morning and had forgotten to lock it properly. Allison was too scared to be grateful for her good fortune and she jumped into the driver's seat, slammed the door behind her and flicked the lock down.

Within seconds of her reaching safety the mucus-crazed little zombie had pressed himself up against the window of the car and started banging on the glass with his arms and head. All the time his nose was running with a constant stream and occasionally he'd blow snot bubbles out of one of his nostrils.

He thumped on the glass between sneezes and he sprayed the window with saliva. Sheets of thick sticky mucus trailed down the glass and his clawing fingers smeared the mess.

Allison searched madly for the keys, in the vain hope the teacher had left them under the sun-visor, as people do on the television but this time she wasn't so lucky. The vicious little snot zombie outside had picked up a large rock and was now banging on the glass with it. Sharp cracks echoed loudly with each blow.

Allison pulled up on the handbrake, pressing down on the button at the same time and the car rolled forward, slowly gaining momentum. Allison turned the steering wheel to guide the car out of the car park; it bounced over the little ramp and rolled downhill across the playground, leaving the gruesome schoolboy stumbling behind.

Allison had never driven a car, or even steered one before and it was much harder than it looked. Without the keys in the ignition the power steering wasn't engaged and the car was heavy and unwieldy. She pulled down hard to the left to turn away from the trees but the wheel lock clicked in place and steering wheel stuck hard; she couldn't turn it an inch.

She turned to glance out of the rear window. She saw the bogie-boy relentlessly staggering after her, arms outstretched and trails of snot dripping down from his nose; a glazed, subhuman expression drawn across his face.

Allison turned to the front again but it was too late; the car was fast approaching the clump of trees at the bottom of the playground and she now had no control over it. She tried to turn the steering wheel hard right but it had no effect. She flung herself down against the passenger seat as the car broadsided with the largest tree, gouging and scraping dents along the body.

She turned again and growling creature was closing in. Allison thought about George and this bogie-hungry monster ripping at his nose with his fingernails; she jumped out of the car and ran toward the edge of the playground.

'Bogggggiiiieeeeeesssss' was the grunting that followed her.

It was darker and shaded in this corner of the playground, the low sunlight slowly filtering through the branches. Allison crept behind a tree and carefully peered out. The boy with black eyes and pale grey skin was clawing at the car window; didn't he realised she climbed out? He didn't look well, he wasn't thinking clearly. His movements were slow and jerky, as if every action was a chore yet he was driven by one pulsating desire.

'Bogggiiiieeeeesss!'

The sleeves of his crumpled black blazer were streaked with long snail trails of slime and his dirty fingernails were caked with grime. Allison breathed heavily, panting hard to catch her breath, determined that those hands were not about to claw at her face. She turned to the school boundary wall five metres behind her; could she make it in time?

She looked back to the car. The small, infected boy was now licking the window where he'd smeared his snot back in the car park; his face and mouth pressed up against the cold glass and his tongue slurping up the mush.

Allison saw her chance. She turned and ran silently over to the school wall, her bare feet scratching on the wooded ground. In one swift movement she leapt over the wall with a low, flat swing and landed with her back against the stonework. She paused for a second, listening for those staggering footsteps to follow her but all she hear was sloppy, wet slobbering.

Carefully she popped her head back up over the wall and the gory little schoolboy was still licking his own snot from the car, as if he'd lost her scent and was settling for the next best thing.

She slumped back down against the wall and saw she was now in the empty car park of the shopping centre next door to the school. The wide expanse of tarmac didn't provide much shelter or any hiding places at all and it was only a matter of time before the yucky little kid caught up with her.

Off at the corner of the shopping centre, an emergency exit door slowly opened and a voice yelled 'Quick, get in here!'

Allison didn't need asking twice as she ducked low and sprinted over the car park. As she approached the door opened wider and she threw herself through the opening and it slammed shut behind her.

Breathlessly, she looked up. Her rescuer had jet black hair which was platted into neat lines of cornrow pleats with little green and red beads at the end of each stump of hair, his eyes were mahogany brown and his skin was dark chocolate. He was slightly older than Allison and he reached out his hand to help her up, saying…

'Hi, I'm Ben Huss.'

40

Chapter 7 – Not Exactly a Barrel O' Laughs

So whit was I doing, when all these shenanigans were going on, I hear you ask. Well I wasn't exactly twiddling ma thumbs, ye know. I knew aboot this stuff, sort of. I was already on the case.

Ye see, George might've told you I was a pipe band Sergeant major in the army, which is technically true but the army doesn't pay good wages to guys just to polish their trumpets. We had other jobs as well. Some of the bandsmen were medics, some were stretcher bearers whilst one or two of us were undercover spies.

That was me, the last one, before I retired. I worked for the Scottish Intelligence and occasionally I'd get sent on these secret missions, which coincidentally just happened to be where the pipe band was performing so if you see an army band on the telly in another country, you've got to ask yourself, whit else are they doing there?

This is, of course, completely top secret but I don't mind telling you because you'll forget everything you've read once you close these pages. I had one of the highest clearances in the country at one point, mainly due to that episode out in the Nevada desert in 1947 with those aliens. Ye see, it's not actually called Area 51. It's a disguised codename which should really read Area SI. That stands for Scottish Intelligence. The Yanks named their base after me but I suppose that was the least they could do considering what I'd done with yon space craft and those stray nuclear missiles. That could've been messy.

Anyway, about a week ago, with my high security clearance and all, the army asked me to help them with a wee job. They wanted to keep this 'little mishap' completely under wraps; they knew how discreet I can be and because I was a local I knew the area pretty well.

Ye see, they'd lost one of the barrels of toxic waste from a research facility near Little Pumpington. I'd heard some stories about the tests they carried oot up there and to be honest, I was thinking about moving hoose. Who wants to live next to a bunch of mad scientists?

And I mean really, how can you lose a barrel of mutagenic chemical?!

Apparently this stuff was called Trioxin and they'd been testing it up at their laboratories. Really heavily guarded place too, so you know something mad goes on in there. The Center for Disease Control (CDC) in Atlanta, USA had identified Trioxin as one of the basic elemental properties for life; an energy force found in all living organisms completely harmless on its own but when consumed in large enough quantities it becomes highly addictive. Agitated little laboratory rats had been known to chew through the bars of their cages just to feast on little nuggets of pure Trioxin.

With a wee bit of deduction and a check over their transport records, I'd quickly tracked down the missing barrel to Little Lake Pump, and I'd seen the spillage and the contamination of the water supply. The water seemed fine but it was the vegetation around the pond that I was concerned with. The plants surrounding the lake were producing a greenish yellow fluid that was oozing from the stems and leaves.

I'd never seen anything like this before and felt totally oot of my depth so I called in the help of an expert. Dr Nobby Allegro was a leading scientist at a university near Edinburgh, working in a small department called the Zombie Institute of Trioxin Studies. Upon hearing of the chemical spill Dr Nobby had travelled down to Little Pumpington the very next day.

Dr Nobby was a pale, thin man with thick horn-rimmed

glasses and a white lab coat. The skin on his face was pock marked and dimpled. His finger nails were bitten down and his hair was lank and greasy. 'Delighted to meet you,' he'd said but I didn't believe him. He wasn't much of a 'people' person; I think he preferred viruses and diseases in his laboratory. He definitely didn't get out much but he was keen to get to the source of the contamination.

Anyway, we'd tested the water supply properly and the results had come back negative. The plant life around the lake had absorbed the chemicals but our tests confirmed the slime produced by the plants was non-toxic and non-addictive. Even if somebody wanted to eat green pond algae floating around the edges of the water it wouldn't do them any harm, except maybe a bad dose of the farts (really stinky wind too).

Dr Nobby wanted to carry out a few more tests but we felt sure I could report back to military headquarters that there was no cause for alarm. The contagion had been contained and there was no threat to the immediate population.

It was at that point, when Dr Nobby and I were walking back into town we saw three black 4x4 cruisers, each with blacked out windows, racing through the streets of Little Pumpington at three times the speed limit we knew something serious was going on.

We stopped outside an electrical store on Little Pumpington High Street. They were holding a closing down sale before they relocated up to the new shopping centre and there was a large 50" television set in the window. Although we couldn't hear him, the man on the telly was talking about some 'breaking news' as the message flashed across the bottom of the screen. We stepped into the shop and turned up the volume on the set. The newscaster continued....

"….and the scientific community is focusing on the phenomenon, specifically on the trance-like state that seems to characterize the assailants. We are facing today a dramatic condition, clearly a behavioural disorder affecting mainly children, which doctors at the Centre for Disease Control are calling preposterous beyond belief. They feel that the only reasonable explanation is a germ that has a mind altering effect on its victims. Though how such a germ could've been spread so quickly does remain a mystery."

More black cruisers shot passed the shop, followed by a procession of military trucks packed full with soldiers dressed in hooded hazardous material suits, yellow rubber cover-alls with a clear glass visors and an air-hose reaching round from the back of their helmets.

At this point, I wasn't aware the little snot zombies had taken over the school.

Chapter 8 – Crèche

George slowly opened his eyes.

He was lying on his back looking upwards through the centre of a stairwell, which towered above him. Green slime dripped over the edge of the stairs and pooled in a thick puddle on the floor next to him. The drips were slow and gloopy and long streams of snot splodged down from the stairs above.

'Shhhh, don't say a word,' whispered a soft voice. Someone was hiding in the darkness below the stairs and holding George closer into the shadows.

'Where am I?' he asked, the words not registering in his head.

'Be quiet! We're not alone here,' the voice said and George felt a finger press over his lips. He pulled his head away; the memory of the snot zombie clawing at his face sent a lurching twitch into his stomach.

'Where's here?' demanded George, not understanding or not caring about any imminent danger the voice hinted at. 'Where're Allison and Kenny? Who are you?'

'Shhhhh!' the voice urged with a tremor of fear. 'They'll hear us. Can you walk? I'll tell you everything upstairs. Stay low passed that door and watch out for the snot, it's infected.'

A delicate body pressed against George and crawled out into the corridor. The girl motioned to George to keep down and she crept slowly underneath the glass pane in the door leading to the crèche. This was where the pre-schoolers and nursery children met every day. They had their own soft play area outside and their classroom was filled with mats, cushions and soft toys.

George followed on his hands and knees, eyes wide in the gloom of the stairwell. He stopped at the door and couldn't resist a quick peek into the crèche.

The nursery was filled with bodies. Some were sleeping, some were sucking their thumbs, most were picking their noses and a few were chewing on snotty handkerchiefs. It looked as if the entire school was bunked down on the soft mats in the nursery class. Children as young as three up to the upper school kids aged eleven or twelve were lounging around on the floor.

The teachers kept the crèche a few degrees hotter than the rest of the school and the warmth had clearly attracted the infected children. Their eyes were dark and heavy, every one of them had hideous spots over their faces and streams of mucus drizzled from their noses. They moved slowly and sluggishly, as if it was an effort to lift their limbs.

George saw many of the children were viciously biting their fingernails, clawing desperately at the gunge on their hands. Other children were forcing their small fingers stupidly deep up their nostrils and causing their noses to bleed; the blood flowing down and mixing with the green snot on their faces and clothes. The nursery looked like a spotty, snottery war-zone.

A hand grabbed George's arm back into reality and pulled him towards the stairs. They both quietly made their way up the steps to the first floor and through the double doors at the top. The girl, who was very slim but slightly taller than George, led the way around to the left passing the Primary 3 classroom, then the staff room and over to the next door. The sign read 'ICT Suite – No Unauthorised Persons Beyond This Point'.

The girl opened the door and pulled George into the gloomy classroom behind her, making sure they weren't followed and closed the door. The Information, Communication and Technology class was loaded with computers. There were desktop PC's around two of the walls and a bank of desks in the middle.

Against the door-side wall there was a long, low cupboard and above it were several wipe-dry whiteboards. Notes and email addresses were scribbled on the boards and coloured marker pens were attached by string. In the corner of the room was a spiral staircase. This led to the open-air weather station on the roof, which doubled as a base of the school's astronomy club.

'Right, stop!' said George, tired of being pulled around and now wanting to know some answers. 'Who are you and what's going on here?'

The girl walked over to the large windows and twisted the thin pole at the side. The venetian blinds swivelled and the room was filled with bright daylight. George blinked and shaded his hand with his eyes.

'I'm Barbara,' said the girl walking back around towards George. She opened the classroom door and checked down the corridor again.

'We may be the last two uninfected pupils at Little Pumpington Primary School,' she said in a calm, matter-of-fact fashion.

'What? Infected? No, that can't be right,' argued George. 'Where are the teachers? Where's Allison and Kenny and... and...and...' George's voice trailed off.

Barbara was softly shaking her head. Her dark, ebony skin was smooth and flawless and her brown eyes held George's stare. 'I haven't seen any teachers for the last hour. I found you near the dining hall. You were out cold but your nose wasn't running so I figured you weren't infected. I dragged you around to the stairwell so we could stay safe for a while.'

'But what's happened to everyone?'

'It started in the infants' playground. I'm a monitor there,' she began. 'The little kids were picking their noses, much more than usual, then they began sneezing over each other. Every child who was sprayed upon by one of the diseased kids became infected too.'

'But why are all the kids in the crèche desperately picking their noses?' George couldn't get the vision of the bogie biters out of his head. 'They were biting their fingernails off to get a taste of it.'

'They seem to crave it,' Barbara went on. 'They want to eat bogies, boogers, mucus, anything they can get their teeth into. Yours, mine, anybodies. They are addicted to the stuff and they'll stop at nothing to suck the snot out of your nose. And if you swop snot, or they sneeze on you, you'll end up just like them – a nostril sucking snot zombie! I've seen it happen. The infants' playground was a nightmare. There must've been fifty or sixty of those things standing staring at me.'

'Do you think the infected snots have spread?' asked George.

'Yeah, they've spread, they're …..all messed up.'

'So if the whole school has become infected, why are they all sitting around in the nursery now?'

'I don't know. Maybe they're tired. Maybe they need a rest,' yelled Barbara. 'They've been doing a lot fighting, biting and nostril nibbling this morning. And their horrible spots….urgh!'

George didn't reply. He just stopped and looked closely at Barbara. 'I think I might've seen you around school before?' he asked. 'Don't you have a brother or something?'

'Yes, Ben, my twin brother,' said Barbara, a little more calmly. 'I don't know where he is though. I guess he was in the upper playground when the outbreak started.'

'Hold on….Twins? Identical twins? You don't look much like each other.'

'Well, duh,' laughed Barbara. 'You might've noticed that I'm a girl.....He's a boy? We're not that identical. We don't wear the same clothes or anything. He wouldn't suit this dress for a start. My school uniform is much too....'

Barbara stopped in mid-sentence and brushed her hair behind her ears with her hand. She cocked her head to the side and quickly stepped over to the door. Gently she pulled the handle down and opened it a fraction. That was when George heard it too.

'Boggggiiesssss'

It was the soft murmuring growl of an infected child somewhere off in the distance. Barbara pressed her face against the gap in the doorway. She didn't move, just kept staring down the corridor. Then she shut the door quickly and began to shove the long cupboard across the front of it. The cupboard was marked 'Stargazer Society'.

'Little help here maybe,' she grunted and George began to drag one end as Barbara pushed the other across the doorway. As George pulled the cupboard one of the doors slid backwards and a telescope and a few notepads fell out. George bent to pick them up....

'Leave them!' ordered Barbara, running over to the spiral staircase. 'They're at the top of the stairs. They're coming.'

'Where are we going to go?' gulped George.

'The only place we can go. Onto the roof.'

Chapter 9 – In the Mall

Ben and Allison walked as quickly as they could through the deserted shopping centre. Allison's feet were cut and bleeding and she left streaky little blobs of red on the white, tiled floor. All the shops were closed and locked; some of the outlets were still empty but most of them were filled and dressed and ready for the grand opening. They had posters in the windows and 'Opening Day Bargains' notices all over the displays.

'So what's your story?' Ben asked sharply. His head was continually moving from side to side as he searched behind the seats, litter bins and fake plastic trees.

'I only saw a couple of those snotty kids but they were vicious,' said Allison. 'I don't know what's happened to George. He bumped his head but I just ran. I left him there. I just ran and ran. I left my friend behind.'

'Well, we've both had to made tough decisions. You'd be one of those little ghouls by now, if you hadn't run.' said Ben, in a cold, harsh way. He was rationalising Allison's actions, perhaps to justify his own. 'My sister Barbara's still out there. She was a playground monitor in the infants but I don't know where she is now. Worrying about it won't help her, or us.'

'What's going on out there anyway?' Allison felt exhausted as the adrenalin from the chase drained from her body. Her feet throbbed and she felt she could cry.

'As much as I can work out, Little Pumpington Primary has become over-whelmed by an army of mad, nose sucking zombies,' continued Ben. 'They lick nostrils. They drink snot straight from the nasal passages. Then once they've drunk their snot, they sneeze over their victims and create more of these monsters.'

'But why is this happening?' wept Allison, the events of

the morning catching up with her.

'I can't help you with that one,' replied Ben. 'But we should go up onto the roof to check things out all the same. We can see across to the school from there. Come on, follow me.'

Ben led the way, taking charge through the empty mall, walking passed the endless stream of jewellers, sports and clothes stores and coffee bars. Allison walked behind, deep in thought. She was vaguely aware that something wasn't right but couldn't put her finger on it.

In fact, she was so deep in thought she almost bumped into an A-frame blackboard that was sitting outside the Grind'n'Bake coffee shop. Ben sniggered. Allison gave herself a shake, stepped passed it and caught up with Ben at the doors.

'So why did you run out on your boyfriend then?' asked Ben, as they walked towards the stairwell.

'George is not my boyfriend,' snapped Allison guiltily. 'And I suppose I was scared. I got a fright, OK... but it won't happen again.'

'Okay, okay,' said Ben, backing off a little. 'Keep your hair on. If you say it won't happen again, then it won't happen again. But don't worry, I'll look after you.'

There it was again. That slightly uneasy, disturbing, out-of-body feeling.

'Bet you can't wait for this mall to open, eh?!' said Ben, trying to lighten the mood.

'Sorry?' Allison wasn't listening properly. She had been too busy coming to terms with recent events to pay attention to anything else but now she stopped. Allison was about to put her finger on it.

'I mean you girls love shopping, don't you? Wasting your money on make-up and cheap jewellery and stuff,' smiled Ben. 'You know, buying things you don't need, spending frivolously because fashion magazines tell you to. You're going to love this mall, aren't you?'

Allison shook her head. She couldn't believe she was hearing this and she certainly wasn't about to be ordered around any more.

'Listen, mate,' Allison's slow fuse was burning now. 'We're not the empty headed bimbos you guys seem to think we are! Yeah sure, some girls like to shop. That's why they build these places to begin with, to trap brainwashed consumers into thinking they need to buy everything they see, as if their lives can be fulfilled with materialistic junk but don't paint us all with that brush!'

'And why do they think we need another shopping centre here anyway when we had a perfectly good High St with the same shops as every other perfectly good High St. I'm smart enough to realise these places are all identical, these shopping centres, all the same stores, all the same brands. Cookie cutter consumerism!'

'Never mind those snot zombies across there,' Allison was in full flow now. 'It's the TV people and the magazines and the media that want to turn people into mindless, spending shoppers. But don't class me as one of them! Alright!'

'Okay, I'm sorry,' Ben was shocked and realised he'd misjudged Allison. 'I just thought you'd like this shopping mall. I didn't mean any harm.'

'And by the way, you've been watching too much Nickelodeon TV and Disney Channel. This is England, buster and we call them shopping centres, not malls! Okay!'

'Alright, alright, no offence,' Ben was on the back foot now. 'I guess we'll be alright here, until someone comes to rescue us though.'

She lifted her head and stared at him. Allison may have been tired, exhausted and drained before but she could feel her energy returning now. She was not prepared to hide away out here when George and Kenny and even Kenny's revolting little brother might need her help. She felt bad enough already for running out on George back at the school and she wasn't going to compound that by staying away now.

'If you think I'm going to be stuck out here with you whilst my friends are still in danger then you got it wrong big time, BUB!' Allison was drawing strength from deep inside.

'It's er....Ben,' said Ben softly. 'Not Bub.' He was still taken aback by Allison's fury.

'Ben, Bub, Bob, whatever your name is, I'm not waiting in this soulless dump when my friends need my help.' Allison was taking charge and she felt better already. 'Now let's get up on the roof, check out what's going on over there and sort it out.'

She crashed through the double doors and ran up the stairs. Without waiting at the top, she pushed down on the bar on the fire exit and stepped out onto the roof. She blinked in the daylight and made her way over to the edge. Immediately below her was the school's MUGA, the multi-use games area with the big blue and red fence all the way around the playing pitch.

The nature area was to her left and further off was the teachers' car park. Allison's gaze returned to the little woodland glade and caught sight of the car she'd smashed up earlier in her escape.

The playground was now teeming with dozens of pupils and a couple of teachers, stumbling around, swaying, moaning and bumping into each other. They were all staggering back and forth and zigzagging to the left then the right. There wasn't one of them that could walk in a straight line.

Their noses were covered in snot and their fingers were coated in dried blood. The entire crowd had faces like acne-ridden teenagers, with angry red spots popping up over their chins, their foreheads and their cheeks. Some of the zits had yellow, suppurating heads ready to burst. Allison winced at the sight but forced herself to scan the mob.

Ben joined her at the wall. Whilst Allison was searching the faces of the staggering masses in the playground Ben was staring across to the school.

'I can see Miss Davenport and a few other teachers. They're infected and all messed up,' said Allison searching the gathering. 'But I can't see Mrs Macpherson or Mr Winchester.'

Just then, the kitchen door crashed open and Doris and Betty, the school's two dinner ladies stumbled into the playground, joining the throng.

'Urgh, I'm not eating school dinners again!' choked Ben, pointing across at the green stains covering their white aprons and their weeping boils.

'Who's that up there?' said Allison peering across to the school's second floor weather station. 'Is that George?'

'Barbara!' shouted Ben. 'That's my sister. She's safe.'

'Wait. Who's that?'

'What? Where?' said Ben, staring frantically between funnels and the weather cubes and testing equipment. A small, dirty figure was creeping up from behind the plant pots and the white, slatted boxes in the centre of the platform.

George was standing beside a dark skinned girl near the doorway as the staggering pupil inched closer and closer to them. George was oblivious to the imminent danger as he and the girl stared down the spiral staircase.

'No, no, George! Run, George! Get out of there!' Allison was screaming at the top of her voice. George turned around, just as the snot zombie leapt forward towards his head.

Chapter 10 – The Science Bit

Okay, okay, I know, I keep interrupting at the good bits. I'm sorry but this is ma story, alright.

And I know what happens next so you'll be glad of those wee memory erasing chips in the full stops. Ye dinnae really want to remember what happens next. It's way too messy. Pee and snot and maybe even a wee Malteser of a jobby.

But I need to tell ye the science bit. After seeing those black cruisers, me and Dr Nobby Allegro followed them, running around to the school as fast as my auld legs can go. The army had quarantined the whole school using enormous inflatable tubes to create a perimeter barrier all the way around. They had even blown up inflatable headquarters, a command centre with two large field laboratories attached to create a sterile environment for testing and producing vaccines.

Not that the scientists here seemed to care about finding a cure. We soon discovered it was more about the containment and destruction of the virus than the safety of the pupils and teachers.

Dr Nobby knew the people in the yellow and white HazMat suits were the soldiers and officers, whilst the orange suits were the scientists. Dr Nobby approached one of the science guys and he quickly talked our way into using one small corner of a laboratory. Didn't seem to matter much, none of the military scientists were using the lab; they were all too busy playing with the drums marked 'explosives'.

The science guy told us one of the teachers had been captured trying to escape without being tested for the disease so the soldiers had thrown her into a holding cell inside another inflatable tent. She spent an hour pleading with the doctors, trying to talk her way out of a series of nasty examinations, and she was quick to blab about the school trip up to Little Lake Pump. We began to put two and two together.

The army boffins were doing their own calculations as well. They'd also put two and two together but I think their answer must've been three million, six hundred and forty two....and a half, judging by their response. You see, I didn't think that it was a particularly good idea to consider surrounding the school with five tons of highly volatile explosives.

But that's what they wanted to do, believing it to be the best way to control and eliminate the plague. So they decided to torch the whole school. Once the army gets an idea in their heads, it's almost impossible to make them change their minds.

And as much as I wanted to argue about it with them, they'd just arrest me and throw me in the slammer so I decided to keep my mooth shut and work on the problem quietly. Ye see, it's better to be inside the tent peeing out, than outside the tent peeing in.

Anyway, talking of peeing, I was pretty desperate by now. Ye see, I'm not as young as I used to be and I hadn't been to the toilet since I left the house that morning. So I went to search for the loo whilst Dr Nobby was working away with a few snotty hankies he'd picked up.

You'd think they'd have plenty of toilets in these military bases, what with all the soldiers around but I couldn't find one anywhere. I must've walked all the way around the school inside their inflatable barricade. One or two soldiers gave me strange looks because I wasn't wearing one of those chemical noddy suits but nobody actually stopped me.

I was practically turtling by the time I found the loo. Ye know, turtling, like a turtle sticking its wee head oot o' its shell. Sticking its wee head so far oot that I was nearly touching cloth. I made it to the toilet just in time or there might've been another nasty accident.

In fact, there almost was an accident. The army doesn't invest in very strong toilet rolls these days and as I was wiping my bum I nearly put my fingers straight right through the paper. I had to wrap the next batch four times around my hand just to be safe!

After I'd washed my hands (honest!) I stepped out of the toilet and realised I was in a section marked Quarantine. This is where they isolate people who might be infected, to see if the disease develops. I could see a cell block at the end of the corridor so I thought I'd have a wee look.

There, sitting alone in the corner was that mad old teacher Mrs Macpherson. Her eyes were heavy and dark and there was a drip dangling off the end of her nose. She turned to look at me but she didn't say a word, just sniffed and wiped her nose on her sleeve.

'Mrs Macpherson! Well, well, well.' I said. 'Who would've guessed you'd be caught running away from your responsibilities, eh? You left so many children behind in that school. You were only thinking about yourself and your own warped values. You're selfish, you are.'

Mrs Macpherson growled at me and muttered something under her breath.

'Aye, I remember you when you were a wee lassie too. It's Susan, isn't it? You never did forgive me for reporting you to yer mam and dad, when I caught you sneaking outside with your boyfriend forty odd years ago.'

'Ye held onto that grudge for a few years, eh.' I hadn't thought about this poisonous woman for a long time. 'Then you had to take it out on George when he was in the infant class. Nothing he could do was good enough for you and you took every opportunity to belittle him.'

'Well, now your cowardly ways have come back to bite you in the bum,' I said. 'Running out on a group of wee kids who needed your help? I mean really.'

She started muttering something under her breath again. I couldn't hear what it was.

'What was that?' I asked.

'Bogggiieeesssss!' she said. I still had no idea what she was on about. Remember, I still hadn't seen any of these snot zombies at this point so I had no idea what to expect.

'Bogggiieeesssss!' she said again, louder this time.

'Are you mental?' I asked. Mrs Macpherson was never right in the head but this was going a bit far. I stepped closer to the bars of her cell to check her out a bit more.

BANG!

The daft auld teacher had thrown herself against the cage with a tremendous fury and an enormous rush of energy; her hands clawing, scratching and slashing at anything she could reach. I jumped out of reach just in time.

'*BOGGGGGGIIIIEEEEEESSSSS!*' she snarled, the green snot dripping down her chin.

Luckily I'd found that toilet earlier or there might've been another accident. I left the infected Mrs Macpherson dribbling in her cell, yellow boils of pus beginning to erupt over her face and started to walk back to Dr Nobby.

That's when I bumped into General Mayham and Sergeant Psycho!

Chapter 11 – Seepage!

The zombie jumped flew through the air towards George, hands reaching out, snarling. Its fingernails were an ugly mixture of red and green bodily fluids and there was a savage look in its eyes. George wasn't slow to react but there was nowhere to go. He pulled Barbara back against the wall, splashing against the rain water butt in the corner.

Just as George thought he was about to feel those sharp, bloodied claws scratch at his face the zombie jerked backwards and was dragged down by the neck. The little creature, whose skin had a yellowish, grey tinge, jumped to its feet and ran at George and Barbara again, growling viciously.

Again the infected boy was caught by the neck and yanked back.

Once more, although slower this time, the snot-sucker stumbled towards George and Barbara, who were cowering the corner, until it felt a small tug on the leash around its neck. Instead of being jerked backwards, the zombie strained forward against the restraint, stretched out its hands and slashed at the air in front of them, spitting, roaring and clawing.

'Hey up, George. Fancy meeting you two up here,' came a cheerful voice from behind the weather boxes and the plant pots.

George looked at Barbara, then over to the little zombie. It still scratched at thin air furiously but it was only now George realised that the small creature was wearing a dog collar. A rope was tied to the collar and fastened securely around the railing at the far wall.

'Who's that? Who's there?' shouted George, not keen to venture forward in case he came within reach of the feral child's grasp.

'It's me, you Muppet.' And Crayon Kenny stepped out from behind one of the white boxes smiling broadly. 'And don't worry; you're quite safe over there. Just follow the chalk lines on the floor.'

George looked down at the ground and saw a series of lines drawn with chalk, marking a boundary around the weather station. Actually, marking a boundary around the zombie.

'Let me guess,' said George, staring down. 'The white line is the safety zone, that thing can't get near you if you're this side of the white line.' Kenny nodded.

'The yellow chalk line is the buffer zone. If you stand there, you'll need to be fast.' And George pointed over at the snarling snot zombie.

'And the red line is the danger line. It'll get you easily if you cross it,' said George, understanding Kenny's system.

'Spot on, George,' replied Kenny. 'You've no idea how tricky it was drawing the lines but they've saved me a few times.'

'It's a vicious little monster, isn't it?' said Barbara, taking a step closer to the zombie but staying safe behind the white chalk.

'Oh yeah,' replied Kenny, woefully. ''Except that monster is not an 'it' or a thing. It's a he. He's a boy. That's my little brother Johnny!'

George looked closer. Possibly, maybe once, without the grey, discoloured skin, the dark bags under his eyes, without the spots, without the blood and without the trails of snot (well, possibly still with the trail of snots) George might've recognised the small boy as the kid who wanted to eat sweets in class just a few hours ago. The transformation had been very fast.

'That's your brother!' gasped George. 'What happened, man?' George walked around the outside of the chalk line. Johnny scratched at him but couldn't reach.

'When I left you guys in the corridor, I knew something was happening,' Kenny began. 'I made it around to infants' playground. There were sleepy little bodies lying everywhere, drooling and snotting all over the place.'

'Johnny was sitting outside, looking groggy. None of the children had much strength but a few of them were beginning to growl and spit.' Kenny groaned. 'Urgh, they were drinking their own snot, George. And the more they drank the livelier they became. It was like an energy drink for kids.'

'I wasn't hanging around to see what happened next. I grabbed Johnny and ran back inside. I went upstairs to the first floor without thinking. Then I saw the door to the ICT suite and the weather station,' Kenny shrugged. 'I figured this was a good enough place to hide out.'

'And you decided to tie your little brother up?' asked George, with a raised eyebrow.

'He was behaving a little nastier than before,' explained Kenny. 'My little brother can be a real pain in the butt and I'd seen how vicious that critter in the corridor was, so I didn't want to take any chances. Just as well for you that I did.'

'Yeah, that was a close one,' laughed Barbara, pointing down at the damp patch of George's trousers. 'George was pretty frightened when your brother jumped at us.'

George started laughing too. 'Yeah, I did get a bit of a scare... Hey, hang on, that's not wee. I didn't wet myself. That's rain water from the barrel over there.'

Barbara put her hand on George's shoulder. 'I'm only kidding, George. The teachers use that barrel to collect and measure rain fall. I know you didn't... you know... lose control.'

Barbara smiled and walked off towards the edge of the balcony.

Kenny stepped closer to George and whispered, 'That's alright, mate. I've nearly pooped my pants a couple of times up here. Once, I'd pumped so hard and nearly followed through when Johnny jumped out on me.'

Kenny winked and George chuckled. They slumped down with their backs against the wall. George was relieved to see a friendly face, even if there was a snarling little snot zombie growling just two metres away. Kenny was actually alright, once you got to know him, even if his brother was a drooling mutant and Kenny still enjoyed sticking objects up his nose. Still, everybody needs a hobby, thought George.

'So what are we going to do now?' asked Kenny, watching his little brother thrust a finger up his nose, snot seeping from his nostrils.

'I've no idea, mate,' sighed George. 'We don't know how bad it is out there. What if the whole world is infected and we're the last survivors?'

'That's what usually happens in the movies,' replied Kenny. 'There's usually some global infestation or a widespread epidemic that causes zombies to attack the population. Victims of the zombies become zombies themselves and this causes the outbreak to grow exponentially, spreading the zombie virus and swamping military and law enforcement organizations.' Kenny stopped to take a breath.

George curled his lip and stared at Kenny in bewilderment. 'Say that again in English?'

'Watch a lot of movies, do you?' gawped Barbara, turning around and trying to piece together his words.

'Yeah,' Kenny went on, '...leading to the collapse of civilization, until only isolated pockets of survivors remain, scavenging for food and supplies. The zombies take over the world, leaving small groups of the living fighting for their survival. That's us, George.'

George was still staring at Kenny open-mouthed. 'And what the heck does 'exponentially' mean?

'Well I dunno really,' laughed Kenny, 'I think it means when something grows out of control, faster and faster, gaining speed all the time. And usually for zombies, the response from the authorities to the threat is so slow the zombie plague grows faster than they can control it.

'But that just happens in the films, dude.'

'No George, it could happen at any time. A virus, a plague, radiation or stem cell research that bring dead flesh back to life or even man-made zombies infected with nano-technology. It could all really happen, man.' Kenny's eyes were almost popping out of his head.

'Nano what?' gasped George

'Tiny little robot bugs that take over your brain!' Kenny was ready to explode with excitement.

'Look boys, I don't want to burst your bubble here,' Barbara was pointing across to the edge of the playground. 'But the response from the authorities seems to have been pretty swift.'

George and Kenny jumped up and ran over to the wall, carefully staying on the right side of the chalk lines. There was a massive, khaki green inflatable tube surrounding the school running around the playground and beyond the shopping centre car park; it was easily three metres tall and there were clear plastic windows clumped together at various intervals.

Beyond the green barrier, dozens of black cruisers, army trucks and a helicopter were parked up and dozens of yellow and white suited soldiers were frantically running around. There was a lot of activity but it seemed to be more about crowd control and keeping the rest of the population of Little Pumpington back behind the barrier, than actually rescuing anyone inside the school.

'Why are we still in here then?' demanded George, angrily. 'Why haven't they got us out yet? They should be getting us out; they should be setting us free.'

'Looks like they've set up a perimeter around the school,' sighed Barbara. 'Their first priority is to keep the virus inside. We're not that high up the priority list so I wouldn't expect any rescue too soon, George.'

George stared at Barbara in disbelief. At first, her brown eyes looked sad though not dejected, then a firm determination set in her face; she nodded calmly, understanding their situation and the realisation they were on their own. She wasn't resigned to their fate but she did want to fight it head on.

George looked into her eyes and drew strength from Barbara's strong-minded spirit. 'We'll just have to sort this out ourselves then,' he said.

'Let's do this thing,' she smiled with conviction.

Kenny shook his head. 'Right, love birds, you can break that up. We've got company' and Kenny pointed over to the roof of the shopping centre. Two figures could just be seen beyond the rooftop wall, jumping and waving their arms in the air. They were probably yelling but were too far away to be heard.

'That's Allison,' shouted George.

'That's my brother Ben,' shrieked Barbara waving with all her might. 'How did they get over there?'

'More to the point, how are they going to get back over here?' asked Kenny.

'Why would they want to?' said Barbara. 'We're in the middle of snot zombie central.'

'I've got an idea,' said George, glancing at Barbara and running towards the spiral staircase. A few moments later George was back on the weather balcony carrying two whiteboards, the telescope and a handful of marker pens.

Chapter 12 – Run For It

'They've seen us,' shouted Allison. 'They've finally seen us.'

'About time,' groaned Ben. 'We've been waving for ten minutes.'

'Where's George going? He's run off,' said Allison, staring over with a puzzled expression on her face.

'No, wait, he's back. What's he doing? What's that he's got?' Allison strained her eyes to just about see George hold up a whiteboard with something scrawled on it. 'I can't read it….it's too far.'

'Wait here,' said Ben and then it was his turn to disappear downstairs. A couple of minutes later he was back dragging the blackboard which was outside the coffee shop.

'They had these special chalk pens in their office,' said Ben, handing Allison two chunky markers.

'But the shop was locked up. Nothing's open down there,' replied Allison, raising an eyebrow.

'And I found these for you too. I thought they might help.' And he opened a gift box and took out set of silver plated binoculars.

'I guess they're for horseracing or the opera,' smiled Ben.

Allison gasped. 'These are gorgeous,' she said but… 'Hang on, where did you get them? The shops aren't open yet.'

'Well, I figured it's an emergency and I've never smashed a window before, shrugged Ben,

'You broke a window!!' screamed Allison.

'No, not just a window. I smashed through the door of the coffee shop to get the marker pens as well.'

'Oh, you can't go around….I mean, you mustn't….' Allison was shocked. 'I mean, you shouldn't….' She had no idea what to say next.

'You better take these as well then,' Ben said, thrusting a

pair of brand new trainers into her hand. 'You look like you need them. I hope I guessed your size right, a little smaller than my sister.'

She knew it was wrong to smash windows, break down doors, basically vandalise the new shopping centre and steal things but this was different. Maybe the rules didn't matter today. Her feet were sore and the shoes would help but she still hesitated...

'I promise I'll only smash windows when we are surrounded by zombies,' smiled Ben, perhaps reading her mind.

'And steal things from jewellers and sports shops?' Allison took a deep breath.

'We're not stealing them, we're just borrowing them.'

'How did the 'you' turn into 'we'? Am I an accessory to the crime now?' laughed Allison, with a shiver of excitement.

'Well, possession is nine tenths of the law,' nodded Ben. 'And you are holding them.'

Allison looked down at the crafted shiny binoculars. Her sweaty fingers had smudged the polished silver as she turned them over in her hands.

'I suppose we should put them to good use. My mum will have to pay for these later and you can take the binoculars back.' And she slipped the trainers onto her feet, wincing at the pain from the cuts and scratches. She held the lenses up to her eyes and focussed across to the school.

George was standing with a large whiteboard above his head that read:

'We're Safe....Are You?'

Without taking the binoculars away from her eyes Allison relayed the message back to Ben.

'They're okay. Quick, write this on the blackboard

'Yes, safe. Can you get over here?'

Ben scribbled furiously with the chalk pen, making sure his letters were bold and clear. When he'd finished he struggled to lift the large board and balanced it on the wall. Allison could see George peering through the telescope, which was now sitting in its tripod in the corner of the rooftop. Then he turned and said something to Ben's sister, who was wiping the whiteboard clean. She picked up a marker and began writing.

George took the board from the girl and held it up. It read…

No, Can't. Can you get over here?

Allison turned to Ben who'd already dropped the board back down and had wiped it clean with some spit and the corner of his shirt. She told him what to write and turned back to see Kenny scribbling on another whiteboard as the girl bent over the telescope.

Ben hoisted the blackboard back onto the wall and signalled over to the school.

Too dangerous. Playground infested.

Allison adjusted the focus on the binoculars and stared across. Kenny lifted his white board up and waved it around. At least Kenny hadn't lost his sense of humour.

You Smell! …it read. Allison shook her head.

George had turned, read Kenny's note and started to laugh. Huh, Boys! Now the girl was writing on her board. At least she was taking this seriously, thought Allison as she held up her sign.

We'll create a diversion for you.

Allison turned to Ben to reply but he was still staring over at school. He pointed across.

'Barbara's got another message. Look.'

Allison turned back and held the binoculars up to her eyes. Ben's sister had grabbed Kenny's board and had quickly written another sign. Kenny was now writing on the other one.

Safer if we all stick together.

Kenny now held up his sign and began jumping around behind George and the girl. It was written in red marker pen and had a couple of love hearts drawn in the top corners.

George fancies Barbara! ...it read.

Through the binoculars Allison saw George had turned, read it and began pulling at Kenny's arms to bring it down. Kenny was laughing and desperately trying to keep the sign up in the air with one hand whilst holding off George with the other. Then they dropped out of sight and Allison imagined the two boys rolling around on the floor, fighting over the whiteboard.

Still looking over, Allison saw the girl look down at the ground then back across to the shopping centre. She shook her head and shrugged. Allison knew what she was thinking. Grow up, boys!

'I think your sister has an admirer,' said Allison, turning back to Ben who was preparing the large blackboard for their next message.

'Well, he'd better be rich. Barbara has expensive tastes,' replied Ben, rolling his eyes.

For the next few minutes Allison and Ben relayed their messages over to the school, whilst Ben's sister had taken charge of the two errant schoolboys and was now coordinating their sign writing. Allison admired how the older girl kept George and Kenny busy, realising that was the best way to keep them out of mischief. George did look keen to help but Allison could see Kenny's assistance was grudged.

Finally, as Allison watched, George and Kenny held up their last two boards together. The first one read…

Wait in the car park
In 30 minutes.

And the other one said…

We'll launch a diversion.

Chapter 13 – Orders!

I couldnae believe it, man! Those blooming army eejits were only going to torch the school.

General Mayham was an officious little nutcase, so full of his own self-importance he didn't listen to anyone roond aboot him – the very worst type of general. And I'd met a few.

Trouble was I nearly stood on him. I'm not tall myself but this little pip squeak was lucky if he was any bigger than five foot nothing. And he was suffering from one of the worst cases of 'Small Man Syndrome' I've ever seen. Ye must've heard of that; it's when a little man thinks he has to act bigger and harder and madder than the rest of the world because his bum is closer to the floor than everyone else's.

Like small dogs, they need to make more noise to make up for their lack in stature; like yappy little dogs that grow out of rich women's armpits. If I put my fingers too close to General Mayham, he'd certainly try to bite them off.

And they take everything as a challenge, an insult to their manhood and they want to drag everybody down to their level with their over-the-top behaviour, and to reach over the top, they usually need to stand on a chair.

Well, me and General Mayham got off on the wrong foot. I was taller than him for a start. Then I bumped into him in the corridor – not good. We were both striding along in opposite direction when we met at the corner – head to head. Or head to chin, rather. I almost squished him.

By the time his Sergeant had dragged me off him I'd broken his stick and flattened his cap. He wasn't impressed.

And his Sergeant wasn't much better. In contrast to the General, the Sergeant was huge, as if deliberately chosen to make the General look smaller. The name 'Simon' was printed above his lapel pocket but I was winding him up by calling him 'Psycho' because he was a nutter too.

Maybe I would've been better calling him Sergeant Sicko, short for sycophant. A sycophant is a bit of a posh word for a boot licker or butt-kisser and that really summed up the big man, since he agreed with every word the General uttered.

'Yes, sir. No, sir. Absolutely splendid idea, sir.' I was beginning to understand why the General kept such a tall man around. It was to stroke his ego – and maybe the Sergeant wanted promotion so it worked both ways.

Anyway, they tried to arrest me first, on suspicion of trespassing. But I soon put them right by insisting the General call the secret service who asked me to investigate at the beginning.

'Phone the Scottish Intelligence then,' I went on until they finally agreed. 'They'll tell you I have security clearance for this.'

'Ha!' General Short Bum laughed. 'Scottish Intelligence? There's a contradiction in terms.' I nearly punched him.

But eventually he did call them and was not impressed when the secret service told him I had a higher security clearance than he did. He huffed and hawed and the words really stuck in his throat but eventually he said I could stay on the base as long as I 'didn't get in the way.'

He stormed out of the office, followed by his obedient little puppy, Sergeant Psycho. At the door, General Mayham stopped and turned on his heel, forcing Psycho to body swerve him sharply, with very quick feet for a big man.

'Remember this,' he snapped, 'I'm still in charge of this operation and I will absolutely protect the safety of the town and the population. I will use lethal force, if necessary to stop the spread of this plague. In fact, I'm quite looking forward to blowing up this school!'

Chapter 14 – Balloon!

'How long is she going to be?' asked George.

'No idea, mate,' replied Kenny. 'I don't even know what she's doing down there.'

George and Kenny were sitting together, slumped down against the wall, occasionally drifting off into silence. Barbara had insisted on checking out the staff room, despite the risks. George and Kenny had pulled the long cupboard away from the door and Barbara had jumped over it, hopped through the small gap and disappeared down the corridor. The boys had gone back up to the terrace to wait for her.

'He's quite happy sitting there,' said George pointing over at Kenny's little brother. Johnny was squatting in the other corner, sooking on a grotty handkerchief. 'It's like the snot seems to calm him down.'

Johnny had been sitting in the corner for the last 10 minutes; quiet, calm and docile. As long as he had a supply of fresh snot, he was perfectly at ease, only becoming agitated when his hankie ran dry. The sleeves of his black hooded top were covered in slimy snail trails up each arm.

'Have you not thought of a diversion yet, then?' asked Kenny. 'Barbara said that was your job.'

'Nah sorry, mate.' George shook his head. 'And I don't fancy my original plan too much either; running across the playground, shouting "come and get my snotters" - just seems doomed to failure.'

'Yeah, I have to admit it wasn't a classic,' chortled Kenny. 'But it was good of you to volunteer though.'

'Didn't really think it through, did I?' sighed George, now regretting his offer to lure the snot zombies away from the playground and allow Ben and Allison back into the safety of the school. 'We should've run across to the shopping centre and joined them.'

'What? With my snotty little brother in tow? He'd be licking at our noses and trying to eat our bogies,' yakked Kenny. 'He'd give us away and that entire playground of ghouls would pile on top of us in a second.'

'But they don't move that fast,' replied George. 'They just stagger slowly from side to side. We could easily outrun them.'

'They'd see us and they come after us. We can't run forever,' shrugged Kenny. 'As much as my yucky little brother is a pain, I'm not leaving him here.'

'Hey, wanna hear a joke?' asked George chuckling. 'Knock, knock.'

'Who's there?' replied Kenny.

'Great big pile-up.'

'Great big pile-up who?'

'Haha ha, you said great big pile of poo!' George laughed and pointed at Kenny. Kenny giggled.

'Nice one. I'll need to tell Johnny when he....well, you know....gets better.' Kenny stopped smiling and looked sadly at his little brother. Was there a cure? Both boys thought about that question quietly but neither wanted to say it out loud.

'Why's he got all those spots on his face? He's like a teenager with bad acne,' said George eventually.

'I dunno, mate. They're pretty horrible,' Kenny screwed his face up. 'Look, a few of them have yellow heads.'

George stared closer. Sure enough, six or seven of the zits covering his chin and cheeks had formed crusty heads over the top of the boil. Underneath the surface there lurked a little reservoir of yellow pus.

'And what's Barbara doing anyway? She's been away for ages.'

'Well, some of us need to come up with a proper diversion.' Barbara had appeared at the top of the stairs again.

She was carrying a large silver bag, a box, some string, a metal canister, a packet of tissues and catapult.

'What's all that stuff for?' asked George.

'Hey, that's my catapult,' shouted Kenny. 'Where did you find that?'

'In the staffroom, of course,' she replied.

'Oh yeah, Mr Winchester confiscated it a few weeks ago,' said Kenny sheepishly.

'You did break a window, you Muppet,' laughed George.

'I was aiming for a tree,' replied Kenny. 'I think the wind must've diverted it.'

'Wind?' exclaimed George, 'Fifty farting elephants couldn't divert a stone in flight.'

'Well, I hope your aim has improved,' said Barbara, setting the canister down. 'This other stuff came from the weather cupboard down stairs. Now help me get this balloon blown up.'

George was first to jump across to Barbara and Kenny made a face at him. George saw that the bag wasn't a bag at all but a large shiny balloon. It looked very fragile so he picked up the canister instead. It was marked with the word 'Helium' on the label. Barbara held the balloon in both hands and stretched the end over the nozzle as George turned the red tap. There was a gentle hiss and the balloon began to inflate slowly.

'Now this is a special foil weather balloon,' explained Barbara. 'It's pretty strong and should normally be able to go up to quite a high altitude; we used this in class.'

'It's getting pretty big,' said George, holding his head back in case the big balloon exploded.

'Bit more, little bit more,' urged Barbara before she shouted, 'Now!' George jumped but was able to turn off the valve just in time; by now the balloon was huge.

Barbara pinched the end of the silver foil and tied a knot

around her fingers. She slipped the balloon off and secured it onto the string and the balloon bobbed about gently in the breeze. Making sure she didn't let go she then tied the string through the holes in the cardboard box. Barbara held on tight as the balloon would've lifted the box too and sailed off over the wall.

'George, put the gas canister in there,' ordered Barbara, and he sat the metal bottle in the box. The balloon still bobbed in the air but was now weighted down.

'A little bit more ballast.' Barbara was talking to herself as she moved over to the plant pots and lifted out a few handfuls of dirt to weigh the box down little bit more.

'What's she doing?' whispered Kenny.

'I'm afraid to ask,' replied George. 'She seems to have a plan though.'

'Right, this is the tricky bit,' and Barbara held out the packet of tissues to the boys. 'Blow your noses.'

'What?' said George and Kenny at the same time.

'Blow your noses hard into the tissues and drop them in the box.'

The boys took a tissue each and looked hesitantly towards each other. This was her plan?

'Hold on, wait,' Barbara stopped. 'Kenny, take that tissue from your little brother.'

'But he's happy sucking on it,' argued Kenny.

'Go on, mate. I think I see what she's doing,' urged George. 'If you don't, I will.'

'Oh alright, he's my brother,' and Kenny stepped first over the white line, then slowly over the yellow line. Johnny didn't move. He was too busy licking the trail of snot on his top lip.

Kenny dived over the red chalk line and snatched the soggy tissue out of his brother's hand and dived back beyond all three lines before Johnny could make a move.

It was a moment or two later the little snot zombie noticed that his feast was gone. He stared at his empty hand, then across to Kenny, standing there with the evidence in his dirty mitt.

Johnny snarled and charged at Kenny, growling and scratching. Even though they were safely behind the white chalk mark, all three of them jumped backwards. The little snot zombie reached the end of his tether and he was forcefully yanked backwards. He came again, scratching and clawing at thin air.

'He wants this stuff pretty bad, doesn't he?' said Barbara.

'Are you sure you don't want to leave him behind, mate?' George lifted a fresh paper hankie to his nose and blew hard. Johnny stopped snarling and sniffed the air.

George held the tissue out and examined the contents.

A blob of clear gloop sat in the middle of the tissue. George tipped the hankie to the side and the gloop slid downwards. Quickly, he tilted the hankie in the opposite direction and blob slowly lurched back the way. George began to rock the hankie back and forth, making slurping noises as his snotter bobbed up and down.

Johnny's head swayed left and right, following the gloop as it slid one way then the other. A long trail of drool dripped down from his chin, as his nostrils twitched furiously.

'He's hypnotised by it,' nodded George.

'Urgh, he's salivating over it,' and Kenny stared in amazement.

'That's the effect I was hoping for,' said Barbara sharply. 'Now don't waste it. Get it in the box and start blowing again.' Barbara held a paper hankie up to her nose and blew an enormous raspberry.

It was at that moment that George and Kenny both realised the plan together. They grabbed tissue after tissue and blasted snorts hard and fast until their nostrils ran dry.

Chapter 15 – The Coast Is Clear

Allison and Ben stood in the car park at the side of the shopping centre, peering over the school wall.

The little snot zombie that had chased Allison from the teachers' car park hadn't climbed the wall and was sitting amongst the trees off to their left. The rest of the school's inhabitants were now meandering aimlessly around in the playground, some of the infected amongst the teachers' cars, others sitting against the far fence beyond the MUGA. There wasn't an empty space to be seen.

'I hope they've got a plan sorted up there. We can't move an inch without bumping into one of those creatures.' Ben was scouring the horizon, looking for an opening. The army inflatable tubes rose high and mighty over the car park and playground, blocking any exit across to the road and all the way around. No movement could be seen from this side.

Ben had dragged the blackboard and chalk down stairs and Allison still had the little silver binoculars in her hand. She looked up at the second floor weather station. There was still no sign of Barbara, George or Kenny and the two of them had been waiting at this corner for at least ten minutes.

'What's keeping them?!' Allison hissed, afraid she'd be overheard.

'You wait here. I'm going over to the playground to check it,' whispered Ben.

'Are you mad?' shrieked Allison. The zombie in the trees lifted its head but didn't look across.

'Wait here?' she'd lowered her voice now. 'On my own? That's mental. That's what they do in horror movies, they always split up, right before one of them gets mauled by the monster.'

'Just wait right here,' hushed Ben. 'I want to investigate

something.' And he stepped out from the corner.

'Yeah right, Ben Huss. You're not the boss of me. I'm coming with you.' But before Allison could start after him, her eye caught a glimpse of movement on the rooftop and she pulled him back by his shirt.

'Finally,' she sighed and she put her silver binoculars up to her eyes. George was standing there, holding the whiteboard in the air.

Diversion Starting Soon.
You'll Know When.

'You'll know when? What does that mean?' asked Allison, turning to Ben angrily. 'That's typical of George,' and she grabbed the blackboard from Ben's grasp and started to write her reply.

'I suppose it means we'll just find out soon enough. Wait, there's Barbara.' Ben was pointing up to the weather station now. 'It looks like she's got a balloon or something...... What the.....?'

Over on the roof Barbara was holding up a huge silver balloon. Tied by string beneath was a small box. Barbara held the balloon over the wall and let go. The balloon rose up and as the string tightened she lifted the cardboard box over the edge. The box dropped for a moment until the weight of the earth inside was balanced by the helium and the balloon began to gently drift over the playground.

'I don't know what's in the box but I would say that's the signal,' smiled a bewildered Ben.

And as if in reply George held up the white board again. It read...

Wait for it!

Kenny appeared at George's side with Barbara behind him. She was pointing over to the balloon and Kenny was lining up his catapult, taking careful aim at the silver target. He fired and Allison could see the elastic strap boing forward and back against his arm.

Ben put his hand over his eyes and looked up to the sky. The balloon sailed onwards. Kenny had missed!

Up on the rooftop, Kenny grunted and lifted another stone from out the garden. He loaded it into the sling of the catapult and pulled the elastic back and took aim cautiously. One eye was closed as he looked along the barrel of his arm. His body tensed.

Parp!

The elastic snapped forward and the little rock sailed past the balloon and over the army barricade. The basket of snotty tissues sailed onwards.

'Oops, pardon me. Must be pre-match nerves.'

'Never mind your nerves, Kenny, man. Hurry up and hit the thing before it drifts out of the playground.' George was watching the balloon now, which had been pulled by the wind closer to the teachers' car park. Barbara was smiling and staring across at the military position. There was some movement from beyond the barrier.

Kenny picked up another rock, slightly larger and sharper this time and he loaded his missile into the strap. He pulled back on the elastic and took aim; steadily, slowly and very, very carefully.

Twang!

The balloon sailed onwards. Kenny had missed again.

'Give me that, you clown' and George snatched the catapult from Kenny's hand. Barbara just smiled but Kenny was far from happy. He pushed his arm across George's chest and stormed off in the huff.

This was no time to take offence. George bent down and picked up a small round pebble. He chose his projectile with care and skill, ensuring the balance and the aero-dynamics were just right; he didn't want his shot veering off course. He snuck the stone into the thick rubber holster and felt the weight in his hand.

Stretching his arm out slowly and pulling back on the elastic, George breathed out. He closed one eye and aimed between the 'Y' of the catapult. He paused for a second, waiting on the breeze to drop slightly; taking into account the trajectory of the missile, the wind speed, the arc of the shot and the curvature of the earth.

He fired. The pebble shot out of the catapult and whistled towards the balloon. George was still looking along his sights and saw his aim was directly in line, absolutely straight on target – except....

....a little too high.

The stone sailed over the large, silver target, beyond the barrier and hit an army truck way off in the distance. George had missed too. Barbara started to laugh and Kenny walked back across the wall with a snide look on his face.

'It's not as easy as it looks, is it?' barked Kenny.

'Well, you had three tries. I've only missed once,' snapped George, eyeballing Kenny with venom. 'Crayon, you couldn't hit a barn door!'

'Let's see you do then, smart-farts!' Kenny was growling now. 'And less of the Crayon.'

'I will! Just watch this then.' George picked up another stone, determined to prove a point, his face flushed.

'And what are you laughing at?' said Kenny, turning on Barbara now, who was still giggling at their efforts to hit the balloon. 'This was your idea. That basket's going to fly past the playground in a few seconds and we'll have wasted all our snot!'

Barbara just grinned, pointing across at the barricade.

George wasn't looking. He was too busy aiming at the balloon, still drifting gently across the sky. He pulled back steadily then….

BANG!

The balloon exploded into a massive ball of orange-peach flame. The box of paper tissues was now plummeting to the ground as wisps of burning material fluttered about the sky.

'Whoa!' shouted Kenny, taken aback by the blaze. 'Nice shot!'

'Er, I didn't do anything,' said George, holding out the pebble he still had in his hand.

'Then how…….?'

Barbara was smiling and chuckling to herself. 'I love it when a plan comes together,' she said to no one in particular. Then, directly at the boys 'Look, beyond the barricade. Those soldiers were never going to allow any infected material to sail over into the town.'

George and Kenny peered over the edge of the wall. They could just about make out a small group of soldiers wearing their bright HazMat suits and carrying rifles. A tiny officer with binoculars was surveying their handiwork.

'So you knew I was going to miss?' asked Kenny, a little put-out by the older girl's lack of confidence in his abilities.

'Well, you did miss,' said George, stating the obvious. 'And so did I….but you guessed the army would never permit the possibility of contagion reaching the rest of the population.'

'Somebody had to hit the balloon,' shrugged Barbara. 'If it wasn't you boys, then I'd hope the soldiers would take care of our package. And let's be honest Kenny, you smashed a window so you're not that good a shot!'

'Our snot box!' George leaned over the ledge again. The cardboard box had dropped to earth close by the wooden nature area and was now attracting the attention of several pupils who had been wandering aimlessly around that corner of the playground. They were oblivious to the burning pieces of balloon fluttering around them. At first their curiosity was aroused, then their heightened sense of smell began to detect a faint whiff of fresh snot.

'Bogggiiiiieeeeeessssssss' came the low, rumbling growl and the first snot zombie dropped to its knees and began licking the green liquid on a tissue from the box. He was joined by another pupil, then another. One of the zombie dinner ladies staggered across and pushed a couple of children out of the way to feast on the gift from the Gods.

'Boggggggggiiiiiiiiiiiieeeeeeeeeeessssssss!!!!'

More and more of the infected pupils and teachers began to notice the commotion on the corner and were staggering across in a zigzag, stumbling fashion. Older pupils were pulling tissues out of the hands of the younger ones, who weren't giving up their prize easily and soon pupils were rolling around on the ground, fighting over pieces of snotty tissue. Some stumbled over the writhing bodies and little pile-ups of pupils and teachers formed on the floor.

By now, the whole playground had been attracted to the snot box and every pupil, teacher and dinner lady was forcing themselves into the area to get a taste. The battle for their bogies was in full swing below.

'Not exactly a Sunday school picnic down there, is it?' grunted George. Kenny was poking at his little brother with a stick from behind the yellow line.

Barbara wasn't hanging around though. She'd snatched up the whiteboard and scrawled **'NOW'** in big bold letters across the front and was holding high above her head. George stared down at the corner of the MUGA where he saw Allison and the tall, black boy running across the sports pitch. He was pulling Allison by the hand and George felt a small twinge of jealousy nip in his chest.

They climbed through the gap at the back of the goal and crossed the playground to the main school building and disappeared round to the right. None of the diseased crowd had seen them; they were all too busy feasting on the feeding frenzy or fighting over the scraps to notice.

'They're heading for the fire exit,' said George, aware there were stairs around the side of the building. He ran to the spiral staircase behind him and shouted behind him 'I'll open the fire door from this side. Back in two minutes.'

Barbara nodded and Kenny prodded his little brother with the stick again.

Chapter 16 – More Science Stuff

I'm buttin' in again. Ye need to know this stuff.

After wasting time with that jumped-up little General, I was making my way back around to Dr Nobby when I glanced through one of the clear plastic windows and caught sight of George and some other kids up on the roof of the school. At least I knew he was safe but I needed Dr Nobby to find a cure before it was too late.

Back in the field laboratory, Dr Nobby had been messing around for about an hour with a few test tubes, a microscope and a Bunsen burner. He'd carried out a series of tests on the snotty hankies we'd picked up and he was able to conclude the cause of the contagion.

It turns out the barrel of secret chemical fluid that was lost, that Trioxin stuff, well, it really was only slightly radioactive after all, and relatively harmless.

Harmless, that is, until it's mixed with pond water. And when the green algae around the lake are mixed with Trioxin, it mutates. Radiation oozes out of the transformed plant life. The reaction between the tiny little droplets of water molecules and chemical inside the algae forces the plague to become airborne. The little kiddies go up there on their school trips, sniff in the contaminated particles and hey presto, all the children have caught colds.

Not just normal colds either. Worse than pneumonia and even worse than man-flu. They have the worst case of **rhinorrhea** *ever!! What's that? Rhinorrhea? It's the posh, Latin name for a seriously runny nose. Just like diarrhoea gives you a runny bottom, rhinorrhea gives you a really runny nose.*

Then the snot turns to crust. The mucus in the infected nose forms lumpy deposits in the nostrils, the body's reaction to protect itself, to stop the bug reaching the lungs, but again it's still harmless. .....until somebody picks their nose... **AND EATS IT!**

At this point I really didn't want to know how Dr Nobby had figured this out!

And why did it have to happen to a group of five year olds?? The worst little nose pickers in the world!

They become addicted to their own snot and even more attracted to everybody else's. The trouble is they're tired and sluggish; their muscles ache and they stagger around feeling very unwell, until a bogie boost gives them a big burst of energy.

With me so far?

The creatures are basically just normal people, infected by a mind altering pathogen called Trioxin 2-4-5 and there's no known cure. Once they've started eating their own bogies, they seem to be permanently turned into mad, crazed, booger-eating snot zombies.

Dr Nobby says he's seen this before, in Haiti where witch doctors would use a similar chemical to turn villagers into walking zombies that were then used as slave workers on their plantations. Too much of this chemical would cause paralysis or even death.

Apparently, there's even a documented case of a zombie turning up in his village 19 years after his family buried him. He'd been drugged then dug up by the witch doctor straight after his burial and had been mindlessly working on the witch doctors' farm ever since.

But Dr Nobby says snot zombies are worse and I believe him. It's like nobody wants to talk aboot it, there so much of a social stigma attached to nose picking. Yeah, it is pretty disgusting but loads of grown-ups do it too. You can see them in their cars with their fingers shoved up their noses.

Like we cannae see them!

It's the last taboo subject on the planet, as bad as cannibalism. In fact, bogie eating is exactly like cannibalism, especially to the snot zombies; savagely removing the little nuggets with the fingernails or lapping them out with their tongues, like slurping up oysters or pulling mussels from a shell.

Anyway, that's the science bit. We'd figured it out, or at least that geek Dr Nobby had figured it out and…..

Hang on, did he say no known cure? What about an unknown cure? An undiscovered antidote that's still out there waiting to be found? We had to find it…and fast!

Chapter 17 – S'not Nice

George sprinted round the corridor and kicked open the fire door. Standing there, at the top of the stairs was a tall, dark skinned boy with cornrows in his hair. George stared at him for a few seconds as the boy eyed him up and down. He didn't look much like his sister, thought George.

'George, this is Ben,' panted Allison as she finally reached the top of the stairs.

'Pleased to meet you, George,' and Ben stuck out his hand. George shook it tentatively. 'Where's Barbara?'

'Oh, we're above the ICT suite,' George was staring at Allison now. Ben pushed past him and started walking along the corridor. Allison met George's gaze.

'I'm glad you're OK,' said George, looking down at the floor.

'Yeah, thanks. Me too,' she replied. 'Look, I didn't mean to run off on you like that. I just panicked, with that little freak biting and growling and stuff....'

'Nah, it's cool. We'd better get upstairs,' nodded George. 'It's safer up there.'

George pulled the bar on the fire door and they followed Ben around the corridor. They reached the ICT suite, climbed over the long cupboard, closed the door quietly and pushed the cupboard back in place, blocking the door behind them.

'Anyway, I hear you fancy that other girl...what's her name? Barbara, is it?' Allison smiled with a cheeky glint in her eye.

'Er well, no, that was..... I mean Kenny was just messing around and....' George stuttered.

'Wow, first it was Miss Davenport, now this older girl. You're a bit of a smoothie, aren't you,' teased Allison, with a giggle. 'Eh, George. A Romeo?'

George's face was beaming bright red and he shuffled nervously toward the spiral staircase. Allison was grinning wildly as she headed up in front.

'No....she's just been a good help, really. Kenny's only pulling your leg.' Then, with a sudden realisation, George changed the subject quickly. 'No, wait, Allison. I need to warn you about....'

Too late. Allison screamed.

She'd reached the top of the spiral staircase and stepped through the door onto the balcony. Kenny's little brother had thrown himself full length to the end of his rope and was snarling and scratching as close to Allison as he could reach. Allison had jumped back against the wall and pressed herself against the concrete.

'Hey up,' Kenny laughed, walking across. 'I see you've met Johnny again.' Kenny poked at his little brother with the length of cane from the garden and shouted, 'Get down, boy. Sit!' Johnny just growled, the weeping spots on his face leaking yellow pus down onto his t-shirt.

Allison shook herself, trying to regain some composure. George stepped through the doorway and saw Ben was talking to his sister across by the wall. He didn't look happy. George stepped forward a few paces.

'...and how are we suddenly better off?' Ben was beginning to raise his voice. 'We've just swopped a shopping mall, with food and supplies and everything for this. We're in a snot zombie petting zoo!'

'We're safer all together, Ben,' Barbara was shouting back. Kenny, George and Allison could only watch as the twins argued.

'But what have you been doing over here?' Ben was pacing around now. 'Have you gathered anything to eat? No. Have you made a 'HELP' sign we could hang over the edge there? No!'

'I thought there was safety in numbers,' snapped Barbara. 'I didn't see you coming up with a plan!'

'I didn't need a plan. I was safe in the shopping centre!'

'Oh yeah, typical, Ben. Think of yourself. Wait till I tell Mum what a jerk you're being.'

'We're not going to see Mum, or anybody else for that matter, unless we get out of here!'

'So what do you suggest, Hot-shot?' It was George. He'd walked over to bickering brother and sister and was pointing at Ben. 'Barbara's had all the ideas so far. What brilliant plan are you going to come up with?' sneered George sarcastically.

'See. I told you he fancied her,' whispered Kenny, nudging Allison in the ribs.

'It'll be a lot better than hiding out in a weather station on top of a school, that's for sure,' shouted Ben, turning on George now. 'You've got this telescope? Have you tried to signal the army? Have you seen anyone to make contact with? What have you actually done?'

'We're safe up here, aren't we?' George argued back. 'We're barricaded in and we're safe.'

'That cupboard won't last. They'll be through there soon enough,' yelled Ben, glaring at George. 'And then where will we go? There's nowhere to run to. We'll be trapped up here!'

Allison walked over to the boys. 'Let's not fall out about this,' she said calmly. 'We have to stick together. There's no point in turning on each other.'

'You keep out of this!'

'Don't talk to her like that!'

'George, just calm down.' Allison put her hand on George's arm.

'What's it to do with you? I thought it was my sister he fancied?' snapped Ben.

He was talking to Allison but looking at George, goading him.

'But we still haven't heard your bright ideas yet, smarty-pants.'

'Well, to begin with we get medical supplies from the First Aid room.' Ben was pacing around again, trying to work off his agitation. 'And a white sheet from the sick bed. Then you could grab some paint and brushes from the art store.' He pointed at Barbara.

'And you could make yourself useful by gathering some food and drink from the kitchen,' Ben went on, nodding at George this time. Ben turned and threw his hands up into the air.

'And why are these guys not doing anything about this.' He hung over the ledge now, pointing over to the khaki green barrier. 'We're up here, you morons!'

'Ben, just chill, bro.' It was Barbara's turn to calm things down.

'Chill? Chill!' Ben stomped to the edge of the parapet. 'How am I supposed to chill when we're stuck up here and those guys down there aren't doing anything to help? And those ghouls…..'

Ben was pointing down to the corner of the playground. The crowd of zombies were now beginning to disperse, the hankies all eaten and the feeding frenzy over. Some were sitting on the ground, others were resting against the trees but most were staggering back to the school. Ben marched over to the other corner.

'What are they doing? Why are they…..'

'No! Wait!' George shouted, rushing forward.

As Ben had been ranting, storming back and forth and venting his anger on anyone and everyone, he hadn't noticed the chalk lines on the ground. Not that he'd even known what they were for anyway; Ben hadn't been on the rooftop long enough for anyone to explain.

Johnny had noticed though. He'd stopped snarling when he'd heard raised voices. As everyone's attention had been drawn to the argument going on at the front of the decking, Johnny had crept around behind the white weather boxes and the plants.

Patiently he waited; not diving in too soon, not giving in to the primeval urges clawing at his throat. He waited. Long enough to allow Ben to march into the corner, this corner, his corner. Then Johnny charged. Ben was within reach and Johnny needed to feast again.

George realised this too late. He rushed forward as a snarling Johnny leapt out from behind the boxes. Ben turned to see a small, spotty, snotty figure bursting towards him. George caught the boy in the midrift with a flying rugby tackle which threw them both to the floor. Barbara pulled Ben back over the red chalk line to safety. Kenny ran to the pair on the floor.

But Johnny was first to jump up. He leapt onto George's chest, pinning him down and thrusting his little fingers easily up George's fat nostrils, licking at the bogies and snot he found. George slapped his hands away furiously but Johnny dropped flat onto George and bit into his nose, holding tight with his teeth and sucking away with abandon.

'Kenny, he's picking my nose. Help!' shouted George.

But Kenny wasn't fast enough and the pain was getting too much for George. Once, twice, three times he punched the little kid in the head. At first it felt so wrong to hit someone as small as Kenny's brother but as his teeth dug into George's skin, good manners and etiquette went out of the window.

Not that the snot zombie took much notice. He was oblivious to the blows at first, obsessed with sucking snot. But George's fourth punch shook Johnny back and he let go of George's nose. He sat back and stared at George, eyeball to eyeball.

Johnny breathed in sharply. And again. And again. He closed his eyes slightly.

AAAAAAAAAtishOOOOOOOO!!!!!!

Johnny sneezed violently and sprayed George's face with a mouthful of saliva and snot.

Chapter 18 - Infected

George sat against the wall, feeling groggy and bunged up. His head was sore and his muscles ached. It had been only twenty minutes since Johnny sneezed over him but already the effects were beginning to show. His eyes were dark and first signs of spots were beginning to appear on his face.

His legs and arms were heavy and there was a slow, burning pain behind his eyes. He just wanted to lie down and sleep. His back was sore and his bum was numb from sitting on the hard decking.

Ben and Barbara, Kenny and Allison were standing way off by the door. George couldn't hear them but he knew they were talking about him. They kept pointing over and shaking their heads. They knew, as well as he did, what was happening to him. It was just a matter of time.

Where George sat was only centimetres from Kenny's yellow chalk mark. If Johnny wanted to he could reach over and just about touch George, but Johnny just sat on the other side of the red line, as idle and exhausted as George. His face was grey and his tongue flopped out the side of his mouth.

Strange how he doesn't go for me anymore, thought George, the last remnants of human thought rattling around his brain. It's like he knows we're on the same team now, or at least we will be soon.

Just then, Allison and Kenny gingerly walked across. Ben and Barbara hung back, staying close to the door.

'A'right, mate,' asked Kenny, shuffling forward slowly. 'How you feeling?' George didn't answer; instead his head rolled forward and slumped onto his chest.

'George? George, can you hear us…' said Allison softly. 'George, we just need to ask you something, well, tell you something, actually.'

'Erm, we've been talking, mate and we….er, kinda wanted to suggest….' Kenny stuttered, 'to ask your permission, really. It's just that er…..we think…. that there's every chance, you know, might be coming down with something and we just thought…..'

Allison stepped in. Somebody had to take charge. Kenny was woefully waffling nonsense.

'George, we want to tie you up,' she declared forcefully. 'There's every chance you're turning into one of those…. Those things and we don't want you sucking our snot. You're much bigger than little Johnny and you saw the strength he had when the frenzy was on him, so we don't want to take any chances.'

'And it's for your own good, George,' she went on, 'you never know what kind of infections you'd catch eating other people's bogies.'

'He's already infected,' poked Kenny.

'Well, we don't want him any more infected than he already is,' declared Allison with a finality that suggested the decision was already taken. She nodded her head with conviction to underline the point and waved across to Ben, who was holding a length of the thick string.

Ben was mumbling as he came across '….still think we should dump him in the playground.'

'We've been over this before, Ben,' scolded Barbara from behind him. 'George is Allison's friend and in the same way we're not chucking Kenny's brother into the seething masses downstairs, George is staying with us.'

'And don't forget, George saved your butt back there,' added Allison.

Ben huffed and lifted George's hands; George was too ill to complain, the colour draining from his face as the spots began to glow red under the skin. He wrapped a length of string around his wrists and turned to Kenny…

101

'You keep the little dude under control until I get George secured over by that wall.'

Kenny jumped up and crossed over to his brother, holding his stick out in front. Johnny lifted his head, his sullen eyes following Kenny's every movement, licking at the two trails of green liquid dribbling down from his nose.

'Don't even think about it, bro. I've got a cane and I'm not afraid to use it.' Kenny poked at his little brother, pinning him down.

'Do brothers always fight?' asked Allison, scrunching her nose up at how practised Kenny seemed be at picking on Johnny.

'Usually,' replied Barbara. 'Brothers and sisters too. Ben and I used to fight all the time. Not so much now though. Don't you have any brothers or sisters?'

'Nope,' said Allison, shaking her head, 'George is the closest thing to a brother I have.'

Ben had led George across to the far wall and tied the string to the hook Johnny was fastened to. Ben deliberately tightened the length of twine so George's couldn't move as far as Johnny. He wasn't taking any chances. George slumped down against the wall and closed his eyes, the bags beneath them darker than ever.

At that moment the school bell rang. The ringing echoed round the playground and the swaying bodies in the yard raised their heads. The growling got louder and louder, as they turned towards the school.

'The bell must be on some kind of timer,' shouted Kenny, trying to make himself heard above the shrill ringing. 'It's about break time.'

'And they are all coming back to class,' said Barbara, pointing down at the staggering crowd. 'It's like they still have some pre-programmed memory.'

'Yeah, and they're heading this way. Not good, not good!'

The bell trailed off and Kenny was left shouting in the silence.

George raised his head. The ringing noise had lifted him out of his sluggish slumber. His eyes had a dead, lifeless glaze across the front of them and a low growl rumbled in his throat…

'Bogggggiiiiiieeeeessssssss!'

Chapter 19 – Grandpa Jock Takes a Pop!

Chemically, Dr Nobby had tried everything in the laboratory. I even had him retesting some of the experiments he'd done when I wasn't here watching. We found nothing that worked to release or relieve the infection. Like the common cold, we thought we'd just have to let the virus run its course. The only trouble was we didn't know how long its course was or how many other people one snot zombie could infect in that period.

We might be totally swamped by zombies before the first infected person began to get better – surrounded by an entire population of snot suckers. Imagine; you start to recover, regaining some strength and wake up, only to discover that everybody else was still diseased and you are the dish of the day.

It would lead to a catastrophic collapse of all large-scale organisation. Nobody left to find a cure, nobody well enough to protect the innocent, with small groups of snot-free survivors attempting to protect themselves. Primal motivations like fear, self-preservation and extreme stress would take over. It wouldnae be good.

Over a longer time scale, all humans would fall foul of this epidemic. The main risk of zombies is their population just keeps increasing; generations of humans would merely "survive", grossly outnumbered and preyed upon by the hordes.

There had to be a cure. But our heads were bursting and we needed to take a break.

We went for a walk and I took Dr Nobby down to the quarantine section so he could see a snot zombie for himself, up close and personal, like. He winced at the sight of her.

Mrs Macpherson was in a bigger state noo, than when I left her.

Her eyes were red and heavy and she was licking at the snottery trails running down her top lip. Her face was covered in spots. Her mouth hung open and a puddle of drool dripped from her mouth. She'd wrapped her cardigan around her shivering body and her permed hair was looking dank and lifeless.

She didn't look up when we turned into the quarantine area but there was a flicker of interest when we approached the cage.

Indeed, there was more than a flicker when I picked my nose and wiped the bogie, a green and crusty fellow, onto the centre bar, about eye level. Dr Nobby grimaced but, come on, man; you must've done worse in the name of science.

Mrs Macpherson stood up slowly and dragged her languid body over to the front of the cell. Her wet nostrils twitched and the drool leaked from her mouth even faster. Her eyes scanned the bars, not looking beyond the steel to Dr Nobby or me but searching for her first taste of fresh mucus since her infection.

Then, her eyes caught sight of the cheeky little booger, sitting up proud and perky and she launched her mouth down on the metal and began sucking the life out of the bars. When she finally released her slobbering mouth from the metalwork, my bogie was gone and there was an evil glint in the old teacher's eyes.

'It's like sharks or lions,' said Dr Nobby in amazement. 'Once they get a taste of human blood, or in this case bogies, they're hooked. There's usually no choice but to put the animal down at this stage.'

'Well, I think we need a better solution than that,' I replied. 'We need to save those kids in that school and I have no idea if George and his wee friends are amongst them.'

Dr Nobby nodded. He wasn't as brutal or as simplistic as

General Mayham; we didn't believe in 'acceptable losses'. But we had no idea where to turn to next. I stared into Dr Nobby's face for inspiration.

Mrs Macpherson now prowled back and forth in her cell, waiting for one of us to step too close but we weren't foolish enough to try that. We were certain our only captured subject held the key to survival of the pupils and teachers in the school, if not to the whole world.

We sat down in the corridor, leaning back against the inflatable tent wall, as it ballooned out against our weight. The radioactive teacher shuffled continually around.

'We could take a sample of her blood?' suggested Dr Nobby.

'Go right ahead. Be my guest, Doctor. There's only two of us.' I replied.

'But why are the army scientists not doing this?' he grunted.

'They're too busy filling up those propane tanks. Goodness only knows what they're planning to set fire to.'

'You know, this sort of stuff is more common in nature than we think,' shrugged Dr Nobby. 'Zombie-like characteristics have been confirmed in the animal kingdom too, just not in humans.'

'No way,' I says.

'It's true,' Dr Nobby went one. 'A newfound fungus in a Brazilian rain forest, I forget its name, infects ants, take over their brains so as to move the body to a good location for plant growth, and then kills the insects. We're talking zombie fungus!'

'How does that work then?' I asked.

'It uses some kind of poison, I think,' he said.

'As a doctor, how would you take poison out of a body?'

'Nowadays we'd use a syringe,' he said. 'In medieval times, apothecaries would use a poultice made from herbs to draw the poison out.'

My brain was working overtime but I wanted Dr Nobby to come up with the idea in the same way I had, just to prove I wasn't barking mad.

'And what about when you were a teenager?' I asked. He shuffled about on his bum awkwardly.

'I can tell from your face, Nobby. You had bad acne, didn't you? Lots of spots,' I was trying to stay very matter-of-fact. 'How did you take the poison out of your zits?'

'It was a long time ago,' Dr Nobby. 'I'd rather not talk about it, Jock.'

'You squeezed them, didn't you,' I went on, refusing to be put off by Nobby's embarrassment. 'Hear me out. You squeezed them and burst the pus all over the mirror. Healed a lot quicker after that, didn't they?'

Dr Nobby said nothing. His eyes had dropped to the floor as his mind took him back in time. Then he looked up at old Mrs Macpherson and her face covered in angry, red welts. He raised an eyebrow and turned to face me.

'Fancy squeezing some spots again?' I asked and Dr Nobby smiled.

Chapter 20 – Staff Room

'We've only been up here an hour and we've doubled the number of zombies,' shouted Ben, 'And now there's a whole herd heading this way.'

'That's not our fault!' Kenny had jumped up and was screaming back at Ben. 'That bloody bell went off.'

'I'm just saying that this is not a good place to hide out. We're trapped up here.' Ben towered over Kenny but Crayon was holding his ground.

'And if it wasn't for George, you'd be down there dribbling by now.' Kenny nodded over to George and Johnny sitting together by the wall. They looked grim.

'We probably are in the safest place, Ben,' Barbara added. 'The school's surrounded and there's nowhere to run. I think we need to hide up here until help comes.'

'But they'll torch the school first,' shouted Ben. 'They're not rushing in here to rescue us and I think the army want to cover up their dirty little secret.'

'What secret?' argued Kenny. 'You don't know any government secrets.'

'Don't you go on the internet? Haven't you read the stories about what goes on up at that base?' Ben made a face as if everybody should've known. 'They've been messing around with Mother Nature up there and we're going to pay for it!'

'I told on now, Barbara's right. There's nowhere for us to run to,' Allison said in a soft, calming voice. 'And Ben, I liked your idea about finding paint and drawing up a help sign. That's probably our best chance, before the infected overrun us.'

Ben put his hands on his hips and sighed. Barbara put her hand on her brother's shoulder and Kenny shrugged.

'Okay, why don't Ben and I go to one of the classrooms

for some paint,' suggested Kenny painfully. 'If you two don't mind watching George and Johnny.'

Ben dropped his head down onto his chest and nodded softly.

'Just go then, urged Allison, 'and be as quick as you can.'

The boys didn't waste any time pulling the cupboard back from the door in the ICT suite. They hopped over it before Allison and Barbara pushed it back into position.

First, Ben and Kenny ran around to the medical room. Kenny pulled the two white sheets off the sick bed and laid them out flat on the floor. Ben was raking through all the cupboards and filling the covers with all kinds of medicines, bandages, plasters and gauze, tape and paper handkerchiefs.

Then Kenny pulled the corners together and twisted it into a large bag. He slung it over his shoulder, ignoring Ben's attempts to help him carry it and they headed off, Ben at least holding the door for the determined Kenny.

They continued around the corridor of the eight sided building, veering right each time until they reached the main staircase. Ben had kept a roll of thick medical tape in his hand and when he arrived at the door, he started to pick away at the end. Finding a corner he pulled the tape out to arms length and wrapped it around the handles again and again and again until the roll ran out and the doors were securely fastened together.

'That should hold them for a while,' nodded Ben, happy with his handiwork and he took off around the corridor again.

Outside the staffroom the boys stopped. Not many pupils had been into the inner sanctum of the teachers' lounge – it was scary enough just to knock on the door. Teachers enjoyed the privacy of their own tranquil shelter away from the madness of the classrooms and most pupils knew better than to disturb the sleeping dragons.

'You knock,' whispered Kenny.

'No, you,' replied Ben.

'Your sister's already been here. There's no one inside.' Kenny was trying to convince himself, as much as Ben.

'Okay, okay, don't push me.' And Ben turned the handle. The door creaked open and inside the room was dark and gloomy.

The staff room was littered with empty coffee cups. There were all kind of chocolate biscuits on the table and plastic boxes of cakes and home baking. Magazines were scattered on the floor and there was a large white board on one of the walls. A door to the right had a sign on it that read 'Toilet'.

'Don't these people wash up after themselves?' said Ben, shaking his head.

'And they tell us to eat healthily,' added Kenny, shaking his head. 'But it's like healthy eating stops at that door.'

'Yeah, do as I say, not as I do.' And Ben pointed to the writing on the wall.

Intrigued, Kenny set his improvised bag down on the floor and started to read the messages on the white board. They'd been written in felt pen, in no particular order.

'Leaving present for Mr Meadows – put a fiver in the tin'

'Jamie Torch in class 3A – Allergic to Nuts'

'Kenny Roberts 5C – Keep away from crayons and other small objects'

The cheek of it! Advertising his hobby to the whole school. He'd only been taken to hospital once last term.

Ben had been collecting all the food from the tables and

had raided the fridge for the cans and bottles of juice from the fridge. He piled it all high in the centre of the blankets and was just about to pick up the corners when Kenny stepped around from the back of the sofa and crept across to the other door.

'I need a wee,' he whispered. 'I've been on that roof for a long time and I didn't want to go in front of a girl.'

'Actually, that's a good idea,' agreed Ben, crossing his legs.

Kenny yanked down on the handle and pushed the door open.

'RAAAAAHHHHH!' screamed a booming voice.

'Aaaargh!' yelled Kenny, jumping back.

'Aaaah,' said Ben, with frightened relief.

Mr Winchester jumped out from behind the second door, separating the loo from the wash-hand basin. His eyes were glowing but his face was pale. He was crouching and making tiger claws with his fingers.

'Raaahhh! Raaahh,' he tailed off, rather pathetically. 'Rah?' he squeaked. Then standing upright again he tried to recover a demeanour of power and responsibility. 'What are you boys doing here?'

Kenny sniggered. 'Why were you pretending to be a tiger, sir?'

'No, I asked you first. What are you boys doing in the staff room?'

'We're collecting supplies,' replied Kenny. 'Why were you hiding in the toilet?'

'I wasn't hiding, I was….' Mr Winchester stuttered. 'I mean I was….keeping….erm…. Supplies for what?' he said, changing the subject.

'We're on the roof, sir,' Ben butted in. 'We're waiting for rescue there.'

'Rescue? Good! Excellent idea. Good, well done boys.'

And Mr Winchester let out a long, relieved sigh.

'You're not used to primary schools, sir, are you?' said Kenny bravely. He figured, with the whole school surrounded by the army and infested by snot zombies, now was as good a time as any to speak his mind. 'Not quite sure how to deal with little kids yet.'

Mr Winchester stared at him for a long time before his gaze dropped to the floor and stumbled over to the sofa and slumped down into the itchy fabric. He put his head in his hands and he rubbed his eyes.

'It's that obvious, is it?' he said, blowing air out through his fingers. 'I thought primary schools would be easy. In, out, two or three years and I'd be promoted to a good job in a big school. I've only been here a week and the place is a madhouse.'

'It'll get easier, sir'

'I don't see how. I just can't relate to little people.' Mr Winchester shook his head. 'I mean, you boys are okay; you're almost as big as the first years in High School. But those infants, they're barking!'

Ben and Kenny sniggered together.

'I took the lower school assembly this morning, spoke for twenty minutes about the school's values and aims and educational objectives,' Mr Winchester went on, 'I then asked them if they had any questions. Do you know what they said?'

'No, sir' Ben and Kenny were stifling laughter behind their hands.

'"Have I ever been locked in a fridge?"' The boys lost it at that point.

'"Have I ever been caught shoplifting" was another one.' Mr Winchester waved his hand as dismissing the complete randomness of five year olds.

'"Can I touch the ceiling? Have I ever stuck a marble up

my bottom?" These questions went on and on and I didn't know what to expect next,' Mr Winchester shook his head again. Kenny was pretty sure he knew who asked the marble question and he looked quite impressed.

'I don't have any children,' sighed Mr Winchester again. 'I'm not married and I just have no experience of small people. They just say whatever comes into their heads.'

'They started to stick their fingers up their noses. Then they started to stick their fingers up my nose,' he shuddered. 'It was chaos. They're dirty, snotty little monsters!'

'Meh, you'll get used to it, sir,' reassured Kenny, turning towards the toilet. 'Now if you'll excuse me, I need to use the bathroom.'

Kenny disappeared and closed the door behind him. A few seconds later he was back, drying his hands on a blue paper towel. Ben had slung their supplies over his shoulder and was waiting for Kenny by the door. He looked back over to Mr Winchester

'You can come with us up to the roof, sir, if you like,' said Ben generously.

'Thank you, I will,' nodded the thin head teacher.

'Don't you need the toilet too, Ben?' asked Kenny.

'Er, no, it's alright. I went earlier.'

Chapter 21 – Tight Squeeze

If you're a wee bit squeamish ye might no' want to read this next chapter. In fact I'd probably recommend skipping the next few pages and you can pick up with the kids back on the roof. This bit just might not be for you.

You don't even need to read it. I'll even tell you what happens here without getting too graphic, just for you wimps. Basically Dr Nobby and I find a cure and then we go to help George and his friends. That's it, in a nutshell. No yucky stuff.

Now, last chance, scaredy-cats. Run for it!

Still with me? Cool, I knew you guys could handle it. Oops, sorry there are a few girls reading too. These comma cameras are brilliant, eh!

Anyway, back to old Macpherson. We had to release the poison clogging up her brain and I took my inspiration from Dr Nobby's pock-marked face. He'd been a spotty teenager and okay, it might be fun to burst yer zits but you've got to watch out for infection or you'll be left with skin that looks like the surface of the moon.

Zits, spots, blemishes, boils, blackheads, whiteheads, we even call them plooks in Scotland, whatever you want to name them, they burst if you squeeze them hard enough. And Mrs Macpherson's face was ripe for squashing.

First, I took my belt off. It's okay, my kilt wouldnae fall doon. I can press my belly oot far enough to hold it up.

Next, I picked my nose; as deep and as far back as I could scratch with my nail, until I'd pulled out a huge big green booger all kicking and screaming, like. Then I quickly wiped it onto the bars before that mad old teacher could dive in for me. I stepped back and waited her to wrap her gums around the metal spar.

I didn't have to wait long. Within seconds she was slurping up my bogie and I wrapped my belt around the back of her heid and pulled her face against the cage. What a noise she made, squealing and hollering and slapping her hands against the bars but she couldn't move and Dr Nobby moved in swiftly with the skilful hands of a surgeon.

He carefully pressed his thumbs on either side of the biggest spot on her forehead. I pulled tighter with my belt and Nobby pressed his thumbs together with a 'Pop!' The zit erupted with an explosion of yellow pus spraying everywhere. I thought I was pretty smart thinking up this cure but if I was really clever I would've worn a facemask.

Dr Nobby didn't hesitate and he moved onto the next yellow boil. I closed my eyes and pulled the belt tighter. By the time it was over I was dripping in smelly yellow gunge. Luckily I had enough sense to keep my mouth closed too, or it could've been worse.

When Dr Nobby shouted 'Finished!' he jumped clear and I dropped the belt on one side, whipped it around the other and stepped back. Mrs Macpherson slumped down onto the floor motionless, her face cleared of poison but with angry red craters remaining.

I stuck my finger up my nose again but could only scoop out some runny snot. It ran down my finger as I wiggled my nostril juice around the face of the exhausted teacher. There was no reaction until her head snapped back and she looked me in the eyes. I pulled my hand away as quick as I could, in case I lost a finger but all she said was...

'Where am I?'

'You don't know?' asked Dr Nobby, frightened to hope for success.

'The last thing I remember was that stupid sustainability presentation in my classroom.' Mrs Macpherson's head was rolling back and forth but her eyes looked clear enough. 'Then I felt really groggy and went to the staff room. Then...'

116

Her eyes grew wide as the truth began to dawn on her. 'No, I didn't, did I?' She began wiping her mouth with her sleeve. 'No, tell me it's a bad dream. No, no, no!'

I don't suppose the memory of becoming a snot zombie is too pleasant. We left her there to recover, physically, if not mentally, for a while and set about finding General Mayham. Unfortunately he wasn't as excited about our discovery as we were.

'I don't care what cure you think you've found,' he started shouting. 'That school is to be burned to the ground. My men will be ready to move in one hour. If there's something you need to do, I suggest you do it quickly.'

'Captain!' the little nutcase went on. 'Captain, escort these gentlemen off the premises.'

A tall man strode up, smartly and efficiently. He wore a peaked cap with a small insignia on the front and three pips on his shoulder. He snapped to attention and stared straight ahead but there was an intelligence lurking behind those eyes that I hadn't seen in the General or Sergeant Psycho.

'This is Captain Kommode.' General Mayham spoke as if his vocal chords were being strangled by his bootlaces. 'Captain Kommode, your men have been preparing the flame throwers for a full assault. I assume we have a full compliment of fuel tanks?'

'We're working on it, sir,' said Captain Kommode briskly. 'We're still a little short right now.......'

A red mist glazed over General Mayham's eyes and his face began to turn a deep shade of purple. 'A little short, Captain? What do you mean "a little short"?'

'Er...no sir, I just meant.....' The Captain's smart efficiency was wavering. Small Man Syndrome could spark off suddenly and be rather unsettling.

'Are you suggesting I'm not as tall as other generals?' squeaked Mayham.

'No, sir,' barked Kommode, regaining his composure. 'I meant to say....we still have a few more tanks to fill, sir.'

'Well, you'd better be sharp about it, Captain. Escort these two gentlemen off the base through any exit of their choosing and continue preparations.'

'Yes, sir!' Captain Kommode fired back a sharp salute, turned on his heels and marched off towards the main barrier. Dr Nobby and I followed swiftly on through the inflatable military command centre. Occasionally I stopped to 'liberate' some old equipment lying around the base, you know, fencing mesh, pliers, a bag of plastic cups and other odd bits of hardware that I was sure the army wouldn't need any more.

'This will do here, Captain,' I said as we finally reached the locked exit facing the shopping mall.

The Captain turned to me and drew in a long breath. 'I wish you all the very best of luck, chaps. Just remember what the General said, our attack will be launched in less than an hour,' and he solemnly nodded his head.

'Blindly following orders, Captain, is always the weak man's excuse,' I tried to say this with as much wisdom as some great philosopher. I think I sounded more like a ginger Yoda.

'Do what you need to do, sir,' saluted the Captain, 'and I will do what's right.' And he unlocked the steel-framed door and Dr Nobby and I stepped outside and ducked behind the wall.

The playground wasn't empty but the infected masses were heading towards to the school so we still kept quiet and crept along the edge of the car park, passed the wooded area and towards the fenced games area. It was there that we would make our stand.

Chapter 22 – And Then There Were Three

Ben and Kenny returned to the ICT suite with Mr Winchester shuffling along behind them. Ben knocked on the door. Immediately they heard the cupboard scraping on the floor and the door flew open.

'That was quick,' gasped Kenny, surprised at the speed at which the girls had opened the door.

'We were waiting down here for you,' Barbara said, pointing over to the computers. 'We went online to check out that military research facility you were talking about.'

'And?' asked Ben, clambering over the cupboard and desperate to prove his point.

'And it's a pretty weird place. There's a lot of websites and blogs that seem to think these guys work outside the law, testing things they're not supposed to; illegal experiments and that sort of stuff…. Wait a minute. That's Mr Winchester. What's he doing here?'

Mr Winchester had crept in silently behind the boys whilst Barbara and Allison had been too busy at the computer to notice at first. Kenny had shut the door and pushed the cupboard back securely.

'Hello,' replied the quiet and now sheepish head teacher.

'What about the boys upstairs?' asked Kenny. 'Did you leave them alone?'

'What b-boys?' stammered Mr Winchester. 'You didn't say there were more kids here.'

'Relax, big boss,' said Ben coolly. 'George is a friend and Johnny is his brother. No problem.'

'Er well, one slight problem, sir,' twitched Kenny, trying to put it as delicately as he could. 'Erm, they just happen to be zombies.'

'ZOMBIES?!' squealed Mr Winchester. 'That's it! I'm outta here. I'm going. Don't stop me now!'

'Look, sir. They're fine' reassured Allison, coming across to him with her hands out in a calming motion. 'They're tied up and quite docile, as long as we feed them snotty hankies now and again.'

The colour had drained from Mr Winchester's face and he was wringing his hands together and nervously glancing up to the top of the spiral staircase.

'So before I forget, sir,' added Kenny, 'I've marked out a few lines on the ground up the stairs. Just stay to the right of the white one and you'll be just fine.'

'More importantly, did you get what you went for?' asked Allison.

'Hit the jackpot!' said Ben confidently and he spilled out the contents of his sheets onto the desk. He pinned one of the sheets onto the wall and picked up a pot of poster paint. Kenny grabbed the brushes and handed one each to Allison and Barbara.

Soon the Little Pumpington pupils were each painting a huge letter on the white material. Ben had opened the tube of black paint and squeezed out the contents onto the table. Mr Winchester had thought about objecting to the mess but figured there was much more mucus to clean up downstairs so a little bit of paint up here wouldn't make much difference.

Time and again they all dipped their brushes into the thick, gloopy puddle of paint and quickly coloured in the outlines of their letters. It wasn't pretty but by the time they were finished their message was simple and hopefully, effective. It read…

HELP!

Ben started to pull out of the drawing pins that held the sheet to the wall.

'Shouldn't we wait for the paint to dry?' asked Allison, ever the perfectionist.

'No time to lose,' insisted Ben. 'Kenny, grab the other end. We'll carry it up carefully so we don't smudge it. Barbara, get the door.'

So, with Ben at one end and Kenny at the other, the boys held the sheet apart and worked their way up the steps. Barbara had run on in front and was holding the door open at the top of the stairs. She'd glanced round the balcony to see George and Johnny, pale and spotty, sitting quietly where they'd left them, gnawing away on a couple of hankies.

Allison and Mr Winchester brought up the rear; Mr Winchester's eyes alert and wary as he first checked out the chalk lines on the floor, then searching across to find the two snot zombies safely out of reach. He took a further step to his right just to be on the safe side. Allison stepped passed him and helped Barbara flop the sheet over the edge of the narrow wall as Ben and Kenny secured each side onto the railing.

'There,' nodded Ben. 'Somebody's bound to see it now.'

'Looks like there's some movement beyond the barrier,' said Allison pointing down to military zone beyond the trees. 'I can't quite see though.'

Shuffling along with his back to the wall, Mr Winchester edged across to the parapet wall. He never once took his eyes off George and Johnny but he was desperate to see if help was coming. Allison had pulled out her silver binoculars and was adjusting the focus to get a better look.

'Are you sure they're safe?' Mr Winchester whimpered, pointing across at the pathetic pair.

'They're fine, Mr Winchester,' sighed Barbara.

'Mr Winchester?' asked Allison. 'You're taller than all of us. Can you see what's going on over the barrier? Use these if it helps.' And she handed her headmaster the binoculars. He looked down at them, looked at Allison then turned to see George and Johnny, still infected, still sitting quietly by the far wall.

The Headmaster took the binoculars and peered through them. He twisted the wheel in the centre to adjust the focus.

'They're preparing for something,' he said. 'It looks like a squad of men. They're lining up.'

Mr Winchester scanned the barrier, across by the teachers' car park and down to the trees. The playground was still infested by the infected, who were crowding round the school and bumping into the walls. Their noses were dripping snot now and the playground had green trails of slime dragging all around.

'What's that down there?' Mr Winchester dropped the binoculars and waved over to the games pitch. They all peered down. A shock of tufty ginger hair could be seen bobbing up and down on the other side of the school's perimeter wall.

'That's Mr Jock,' yelled Allison. 'I'd recognised that red hair anywhere.'

'Give me a closer look.' And Mr Winchester crept closer to the wall, taking care not to step over the white safety line. He pulled the glasses up to his eyes and watched as tools and rolls of wire were thrown over the fence into the MUGA.

'I think he's..........'

'BOGGGGIIIIIEEEEESSSSSSS!!!!'

BAM!

Mr Winchester was thrown to the side. He bounced and rolled into the corner, banging his head against the wall on the way down and knocking him unconscious. George was on him in a second, snarling and spitting as he clawed at the Headmaster nose, feasting on the fresh bogie.

'George is loose!' screamed Allison, running to the back of the weather deck. Ben and Barbara jumped clear as Kenny ran towards his little brother, keeping him at bay with his stick. He looked down at the rope used to tie George. The end was saturated with snot and it had been chewed clean through.

'He's bitten through the rope,' yelled Kenny

'Do something,' Allison shrieked again.

'I'm going nowhere near him,' shouted Ben. 'Who wants that disease?'

Mr Winchester was lying on the ground, unflinching and perfectly still. George was kneeling on his chest, clawing mucus from the headmaster's nose before licking his fingers in turn. His breathing was slow and shallow and he appeared to be enjoying the feast.

AAAAAAAAAAATISHOOOOOOOO!

George sat upright; his heavy eyelids streaming as the sneeze caught him by surprise.

AAAAAAAAAAATISHOOOOOOOO!

He sneezed again and spat a huge gob of phlegm into Mr Winchester's face. The Headmaster didn't move.

'I don't think we can stay here,' said Ben creeping towards the door.

Kenny was backing away from his growling brother, occasionally poking him with the cane. 'I'm with you on that,' he said without looking over his shoulder.

'You can't leave little Johnny here,' squealed Allison. George lifted his head at the sound.

'I don't want to,' Kenny shouted back, 'but when Mr Winchester comes around, we're going to have three snot zombies up here and two of them will be loose.'

'We could tie them up,' suggested Barbara, her voice shrill and desperate.

'How can we get close to George without him sneezing on us?' argued Ben. 'I reckon we leave them up here, head over to the barricade and wait for the army to come in. They're getting ready for something down there and they must've seen our 'help' sign.'

'Bogggiiiiieeessssss!'

George was eyeing up Allison now, who was closest to the Headmaster's slumped body. George had a long trail of drool dripping down from his mouth; he dropped his hands onto the ground and began crawling on his hands and knees towards her.

'I think we'd better get out of here,' Ben urged.

'I think you might be right. Easy now, nice and slow.' Allison was shuffling backwards not taking her eyes off her infected friend.

Atishoo!

Mr Winchester sat bolt upright, clear snot dripping from his nose. His skin was pale and dark bags were beginning to form under his eyes.

'NICE AND SLOW, MY BUTT!' screamed Kenny as he ran passed Allison, Ben and Barbara. He stopped for a second and opened the door at the top of the staircase. Pushing it wide, he ran down the steps two at a time, quickly followed by the other three.

Once they were out of the ICT suite the four of them ran left around to the fire exit and down the external stairs. The MUGA was straight in front of them but they weren't prepared for the sight in front of them in the playground.

Chapter 23 – Sea of Green

The playground was awash with snot. It hadn't been obvious from their high vantage point but now down at ground level everything was dripping with slime.

Allison and Kenny were first to edge forward from the staircase. Trails of green slithered across the playground and they stepped carefully to avoid falling. It was like walking on ice.

The rest of the playground opened up behind them as they inched forward. Round to their left and behind the staircase, infected pupils and teachers could be seen staggering about, no control over their heavy limbs. Many of them were sliding around in pools of their own snot, unable to right themselves.

Straight ahead Allison caught sight of two figures working furiously in the MUGA. One was wearing a green and red kilt and sported a crown of ginger hair; the other wore a long white coat.

'Mr Jock!' yelled Allison, waving furiously.

'Shhh!' We don't want those things to hear us,' hushed Barbara but Grandpa Jock had heard them already and was beckoning them frantically to come over. Allison led the way, slipping through the snotter, like Bambi on ice. Kenny came sliding up with a professional glide across the greasy surface. Ben and Barbara followed on without really knowing where they were going.

'Roond the side, lass,' waved Grandpa Jock as she approached the games area. Behind the goals closest to the school Grandpa Jock was working away with the pliers and a set of wire-cutters as the other man held the mesh fence panels in place.

'I've no' fixed that side yet. Ye can get in over there.' And Grandpa Jock signalled over to the other goal near the trees. 'And ye better hurry because those freaks have heard you.'

Allison turned to see a slow, swaggering wave of infected pupils rolling towards them, their noses streaming. She darted to her right and ran towards the other end of the MUGA. The other three gave chase, hoping the mad old Scotsman had a real plan.

Allison saw the gap in the side of the white goal and she clabbered through. Grandpa Jock was there within seconds.

'In you get, Crayon, lad,' Grandpa Jock encouraged Kenny and then he held out his hand for Barbara, then Ben. Ben looked twice before accepting help.

'This is George's grandfather,' explained Allison to Ben and Barbara as they made their hurried introductions. Grandpa Jock wrapped the fence wire around the gap in the goals and began twisting and sealing the mesh onto the goal frame. With a few twists of his pliers the hole was secured and he stepped back to view his handiwork.

'We're safe in here noo. Speaking of George, where is he, lass?' Grandpa Jock's face was grim.

'Oh Mr Jock, we couldn't help it,' sighed Allison. 'He took a sneeze full in the face and he's one of them now.'

'Aye, I feared the worst,' nodded Grandpa Jock grimly, 'when I didn't see him come down the stairs with you. Still, this is Dr Nobby and we think we've found a solution. We'll sort him out later.'

The man in the white lab coat came trotting up at that point. 'The door is sealed and it's all secure at that side too. We're safely trapped in here now.'

'Hehehe,' chuckled Grandpa Jock. 'Bring on the snot zombies!'

Kenny looked fearfully at Allison as they surveyed their surroundings. They'd all played football, basketball and netball inside the games area many times but they'd never seen it like a prison before.

'We're in a cage!' shouted Barbara. 'We're trapped in a cage and we're about to be surrounded by the snot suckers.'

'That's what we're hoping for!' laughed Grandpa Jock.

'You think this is funny?' barked Kenny, waving his arm at the hordes of pale pupils stumbling towards them. 'We're bait!'

'This is your fault, Kenny. You and your zombie mate, George!' Ben was screaming now, the walls of their prison closing in around them as zombies approached. He was about to punch Kenny in the arm before Grandpa Jock pressed down on his shoulder.

'Calm down, boyo, calm down. We're all in this together,' reassured Grandpa Jock. 'We can't let personal feelings and petty arguments get in the way of oor survival.'

'So what do you suggest, old man?' Ben was snarling at Grandpa Jock now, turning his attention away from Kenny.

'Me and the doctor think we've found a cure,' Grandpa Jock hesitated, 'but it might get messy. Here, put these on.' And he threw across a bag of what looked like white plastic cups with elastic strings to Kenny.

'What are these?' asked Kenny, pulling the first mask out of the bag.

'These, my young crayon-loving friend, are known as surgical barrier masks, the very best the army and our taxes can afford.' Grandpa Jock lifted one and stretched the elastic over his head.

'A moulded face mask with outer splash repellent layer,' he went on, 'and a highly efficient bacterial filtration system. Look, it says so there.' And Grandpa Jock pointed to the label.

'They are very good for work in the lab, Jock' agreed Dr

Nobby, pulling his over his head. 'They also have a soft tissue inner layer for sensitive skin but I'm not sure we're too worried about that now.'

The fence around the games area was now totally surrounded by the infected. They were pressing in and stretching their arms through the bars. Faces were crushed up against the metal as their filthy hands clawed at thin air in front of them. Zombies of all sizes were forcing themselves against the cage walls, growling, drooling and dripping over the synthetic floor.

'Boggggiiiiieeeessssss!'

'Heh heh, Nobby, bring your sensitive skin over here now,' ordered Grandpa Jock with a smile. 'We have a job to do. Look and learn, kids.'

'Boggggiiiiieeeessssss!' groaned the seething mass of snot zombies.

Grandpa Jock turned to the fence and grabbed the closest little zombie by the ear and pulled him close up against the bars. With his free hand he began squeezing the spots on the small child's face and one by one the zits exploded, oozing yellow pus over Grandpa Jock's face and hand, as well as the floor. Once the last boil was burst the small child slid slowly down onto the floor

Dr Nobby joined in too, a little more gently than Grandpa Jock but his hands moving faster across each zombie's face, squidging down on the plooks and forcing out the poison.

Ben and Kenny looked at each other and smiled. They weren't teenagers yet but they enjoyed squeezing the odd zit that had started to appear on their faces. It might be yucky fun to squash other people's spots too, they thought. And anyway, they were at the cutting edge of medical technology; Dr Nobby said so (although he was laughing at the time).

'We might as well give it a try,' laughed Ben.

'After you, Benjamin,' giggled Kenny.

And the two boys pulled their masks down over their mouths and noses and dived in against the fence, picking on the smaller snot zombies with glee. Allison joined in too, squashing the faces of some of the girls in the older classes that she didn't particularly like.

'George would've loved this,' said Kenny, with a sigh.

But Barbara didn't want to join in. She screwed up her face in disgust, pulled herself away from the edge of the fence and walked over to the middle of the football pitch. There was absolutely no way she was going to become involved in administering this type of treatment; she just sat down on the centre spot and covered her ears from the hideous squidge, squidge, squirting noises.

Chapter 24 – Burning Rings of Fire

Grandpa Jock was thoroughly enjoying himself now, grabbing bigger and bigger zombies and blasting the heads of the spots with a ferocious double-fingered technique. It was Grandpa Jock who took care of the two snot slurping dinner ladies and a few of the teachers as well, each one sliding down to the ground in their own pus, once the infection had been cleared out until almost all of the adults and children had been purified.

'Pressi Diem!' he shouted with delight as he squashed zit after zit. 'Squeeze the day!'

'He's enjoying this, isn't he,' giggled Ben.

'A bit too much,' laughed Kenny.

'We're food for worms, lads. Don't wait til it's too late.'

'I think we might be too late, Jock,' croaked Dr Nobby, nodding over to the army barricade, which had been unzipped in the middle and pulled back to reveal a huge entrance. Columns of soldiers in yellow HazMat suits were marching through into the playground. They wheeled left and spread out in a long line between the car park and the trees. One solitary orange suit stepped in front of the column.

'Oh Captain, my Captain,' yelled Grandpa Jock, 'Can't you see we found a cure?' And he saluted across to the column.

Allison wasn't sure if the orange suited officer returned his salute or if he was saluting the dwarf in the black HazMat, who was strolling into the playground behind his troops. He was followed by a giant in a yellow protective suit that was too small him. Three inches of wrist poked out on each arm between the bottom of the sleeves and his tight gloves.

'One minute to destruction, General,' barked Kommode.

'Carry on, Captain!'

'We better get a move on, people,' ordered Grandpa Jock. He didn't hesitate. He ran to the goal mouth nearest the school, picked up his pliers and snipped off the wires holding the fence panel in place. He kicked it off the stanchion and stepped through.

'We've got to get these people inside now!' he yelled and Dr Nobby raced after him.

'But won't they want to eat our bogies?' asked Barbara, not quite convinced the spot squishing would be enough.

'They should be cured by now,' replied Dr Nobby. 'We've purged most of the poison out but they'll still be a bit groggy.'

'Come on, on your feet, snot suckers,' Grandpa Jock was shouting and forcing the dazed ex-zombies to walk towards the school. 'Kenny, get the door open!'

Kenny hopped through the back of the goalmouth and ran to the rear door of the kitchen. He turned the handle and pulled it towards him. Ben, Barbara and Allison were now shepherding as many pupils as could stand into the school. Dr Nobby was pulling a few reluctant stragglers over to the school and Grandpa Jock was bringing up the rear, carrying one infant in his arms and holding the hand of a crying youngster.

Some of the teachers, as well as Doris and Betty the dinner ladies had come to their senses and were helping direct the flow of children back into the school. They could see the column of soldiers, fuel tanks strapped to their backs and flame throwers at the ready. The teachers knew something was wrong.

The small General in the black suit stood at the side and barked muffled orders through his visor.

'Lead your men into battle, Captain.'

'Twenty seconds,' Captain Kommode roared. Time ticked on slowly.

The flow of children into the kitchen was gathering pace but there were still dozens of pupils in the playground and there was a logjam forming around the doorway.

'We'll all be scorched if we don't get inside,' screamed Grandpa Jock above the clamour of scared voices. 'Nobby, take some round to the other door. We'll never get them all in here in time.' And the pale scientist started redirecting the pupils nearest him around to the soft play area.

Back at the barricade the irate little General was looking furiously at his wrist. 'Is your watch slow, Captain?' he bawled.

'No, sir,' he replied. 'I believe my timepiece is accurate, sir.'

'Then bloody well get on with it, man!'

'Yes, sir,' replied the Captain, pausing again.

'I'm warning you, Captain,' growled the General.

'Twenty seconds!' he bellowed.

'Twenty seconds? It was twenty seconds thirty seconds ago,' squealed the General, his fat little fists clenched in rage.

'Twenty seconds,' repeated the Captain.

'THAT'S IT!' exploded the General. 'Captain, you are relieved of your duties. Sergeant, take him inside.'

And the giant Sergeant thankfully put his hand on the Captain's shoulder and pressed him towards the barricade entrance quickly. Maybe this wasn't a pretty place to be and the Sergeant seemed pleased to be leaving the scene of the crime. The Captain was hoping his delay had bought them enough time.

'Now to cover up this mess properly,' muttered the General as they filed passed him.

'I'm taking charge now, men. Light ignitions,' ordered the General, throwing his shoulders back fiercely.

The flames on the gun barrels click on with a bright blue pilot light as each of the soldiers dropped their weapons into the 'ready' position. The General was twitching with rage but stared down the line of his troops, ready to bring destruction down on the school and cover up the military's dirty secret.

'Five seconds! Prepare to fire.'

The soldiers, spread across the playground at three metre intervals, scanned the area of their assault. They'd trained for this; prepared and drilled incessantly to protect their country unquestioningly and now that moment had arrived.

'Take no prisoners. Leave no infected area untouched. In three…'

'Two'

'One. Fire!'

Jets of searing hot flame shot from the muzzle of each weapon. The soldiers in the HazMat suits began moving forward in a sweeping motion, blasting long arcs of blazing liquid across the playground.

137

Chapter 25 – Remember, Don't Forget.

And ye know that's how all zombie stories end.

Death, devastation, civilisation destroyed, zombies running amok, innocents caught up in the senseless destruction and when the authorities finally decide to act it's usually too late and only to cover up their own faults and failings. Their reaction is always extreme and everybody wiped out in the end.

Heh heh, except this time, ya cheeky bandits!

Ye see, their flamethrowers wouldnae work. They tried to fireball the school and sure enough, jets of flame were sprayed all over the playground and the walls and the school itself but the whole place was too gooey!

With all that snot and spot spurt oozing over everything the school was just too soggy to burn. The army tried hard enough; they blasted the building until their fuel tanks ran dry but they'd only just managed to burn off the first layer of slimy crust. And by then me and Dr Nobby had got all the pupils into the safety of the school gardens in the centre of the octagon.

I made a quick phone call to the top brass at the army, the guys who asked me to investigate the missing barrel of toxic chemical in the first place, and told them all about General Mayham's eccentric behaviour. I mean, the man just wouldn't listen to reason. It was his squadron that had lost the barrel in the first place and he was just covering up his tracks…

…Aye, by burning down a school and all the pupils! As if nobody would notice?!

Anyway, the real army showed up and took control from that mad little General and began the clear up operation with the help of the teachers, the dinner ladies and Barbara. She was brilliant with the little kids, teaching them how to blow their own noses properly and telling them not to pick their spots.

This just left one wee problem; George and the zombies upstairs.

Allison took us up to the ICT suite, with Ben and Kenny. Me and Dr Nobby jumped over the cupboard first to make sure none o' them were lurking about in the computer room.

We had a bit of a plan, something we'd learn back at the MUGA.

Before we went upstairs Dr Nobby had ran back to the lab for something. He muttered a load of gibberish about 'conscious sedation treatment' or words to that effect so I thought I would've been prepared when he pulled out two large hypodermic syringes at the bottom of the spiral staircase.

I was so shocked I nearly wet my pants. The needles were absolutely huge!

Dr Nobby nodded. 'Trust me, I'm a doctor.' And he carefully explained his plan and we crept up the stairs quietly.

At the top we all peered out through the gap in the door. The last three infected zombies hadn't even tried to escape the rooftop. They were sitting quietly in the corner, sharing their bogies and nibbling their fingers. Snot was dripping from their noses, mixed with a little blood where they'd picked too hard. The spots on their faces looked ripe and ready to burst.

'They're not going to want to remember this,' I whispered to Dr Nobby. Nobody wants to have a memory about eating their headmaster's snot.

'That's what these are for,' said Nobby in a hushed tone. 'It's a local anaesthetic, brings on short term memory loss. The doctors and scientists are administering this to everyone downstairs. No one will remember a thing.'

'And it will calm George and Mr Winchester down before we can squeeze their spots?' asked Allison, who standing behind us.

'What about my little brother?' asked Kenny, listening in.

'Well, it will slow down adults and older children,' confirmed Dr Nobby gravely, 'but it's too risky to give to a small child unless under carefully controlled conditions. Kenny, you'll have to distract your brother for a few moments.'

And Dr Nobby handed me a syringe!

'Whit do ye want me to do with this!' I screamed. 'I'm no' the doctor. You said "Trust me, I'm a doctor" but I'm not a doctor. You are! Aren't you going to do this?'

'Calm down, Mr Jock,' reassured Allison but I was starting to panic.

'Just shove it into George's butt cheek and press down on the plunger,' explained Dr Nobby.

'And you'll have to hurry, Mr Jock. I think George heard you,' nodded Ben and I peeked through the gap in the door.

'Boggggiiiieesssss!' growled George, now standing up and stumbling towards the stairs.

Dr Nobby and Ben sprinted onto the decking first. George was slow and staggering and they bobbed passed him with ease. Mr Winchester was lying on the ground; he was last to be infected and still a little groggy with fever and the bump to his head. Ben dangled a freshly blown handkerchief on the floor about a metre beyond Mr Winchester's head; he rolled over onto his tummy and crawled towards the new snack.

Dr Nobby rammed his bottom with his syringe pumped the solution into his skinny butt. The shocked head teacher knelt bolt upright, before his knees buckled and he toppled over again. Then Dr Nobby jumped into 'squeeze mode'.

One down, two to go.

Allison jumped around one side of the white weather boxes and I went round the other. Luckily George followed

Allison and he shambled after her. I was able to get in close and as planned Allison crouched down on the ground in a tight ball to avoid any sneeze splashes.

Then in the most ladylike manner I have ever seen, she delicately slipped a finger up one of her nostrils then offered it to George. It was too much for him to resist. He leapt forwards, pinned Allison's hand to the ground and began licking her fingers.

His bum was sticking straight up in the air and made a brilliant target for my needle. Without wanting to hesitate I closed my eyes and stabbed my syringe into George's cheek pressing down on the pumper.

I wasn't impressed with my grandson at that point because he squealed like a girl. But I suppose that's to be expected when a sharp needle is jabbed into your tushie. George rolled over and crashed onto the ground. Partially stunned and semi-conscience George's spots didn't stand a chance.

'Hey, look at this!'

Kenny's job was to keep his little brother distracted long enough for the rest of us to take care of George and Mr Winchester. He'd done it rather well.

I stood up to see Kenny smiling, pointing with his stick at the little bundle clothes running round in circles, slurping away.

'What did you do to Johnny?' gasped Allison when she caught sight of the rag ball.

'He's like a little dog chasing its tail,' I chuckled, as the small boy continued going round and around.

'I picked my nose and wiped it on my stick,' beamed Kenny, proud of his achievement. 'Then I threw the stick into the corner and when Johnny went after it I grabbed him from behind and pulled his hoodie up and over his face.'

'Yes,' laughed Dr Nobby, 'and now he can only see and smell the snot straight in front of him. No wonder he's running around demented.'

We stood and laughed at the little snot zombie for a couple of minutes, then we pinned him down and squeezed the pus from his face.

Special agents from the government arrived a wee while later and wanted to make sure everybody's mind had been properly erased. A medical centre had been set up in the school's assembly hall and everybody was tested for traces of the contagion.

Then just to be on the safe side everyone was injected with the memory erasing anaesthetic, even if they hadn't been infected with the virus, 'as a precaution'. Allison, Kenny, Barbara and Ben can't remember a thing about all this either.

Eventually everybody was released back to the worried mums and dads on the other side of the barrier. The townsfolk had been told a story about a flu-like virus that had affected the school but it had now been safely treated.

And if any parent wants to take their child to the doctor's to explain aches, pains, runny noses and even the strange pock-marked dimples on their little darling's face, every doctor has been trained to say 'It's viral.'

George recovered well enough and luckily he remembers nothing about it; he can't even remember fancying his teacher but I think he's just keeping that quiet . Now and again he'll remember some vague detail about the army coming to his school or the man in the white coat called Dr Nobby, who still visits us occasionally and he'll ask what really went on.

And I always reply, 'Nothing, lad. S'not anything to worry about.'

I managed to convince the Secret Service that I was on their side and of course, I had signed the Official Secrets Act 1992, up as high as Level 36X so I didn't need to get a needle jab in my bum. No one else in Little Pumpington is aware of what went on in the school that day and I plan to keep it that way – George does not need to know he was eating the bogies from his teacher's nose!

And anyway, what are you laughing at?

Little Pumpington wasn't the only school infected by that Trioxin 2-4-5 stuff. My security clearance meant that I could look at the government records and find out about all the other outbreaks that happened when military laboratories began moving their chemicals around earlier this year and I can tell you it happened in several schools all over the country.

Maybe it happened at your school?

You wouldn't remember it anyway because some army doctor would've shoved a needle in your bum to make you forget!

Do you feel fluey sometimes? Stiff neck, sore shoulders, maybe a runny nose now and again? Has the doctor ever said to your mum 'Don't worry, it's just a virus'?

Ever get the strange urge to pick your nose?

Maybe you're not quite cured. Maybe the symptoms are coming back again.

Have you ever had a spot on your face? Watch out for them, zits just might begin to appear.

And when they do, you might just be about to turn into a snot zombie. Once those bolls begin bursting out all over your face, it's only a matter of time before you're sticking your fingers up somebody's nose and eating their bogies.

Heheheh, ya mucky mucus munchers that you are!

The End
(insert final amnesia chip here.)

Epilogue - Grandpa Jock's Guide to a Zombie Epidemic

Un-Disclaimer

I told ye no' to read this book. Now you know far too much and the government is going to be keeping a close watch on ye from noo on.

Can you remember the bit at the start? You know, when I pretend that none of this is real. 'The characters portrayed in this book are fictional. Any similarity to person or persons alive, dead or undead is purely coincidental.' That all stops here! You thought I only put in the word 'undead' to be funny when actually this stuff is real and has really happened and I've even included acknowledgements to prove it, man!

And let's be honest, the only reason you're reading this book is because you're a mental wee nutter who's obsessed with zombies, not just snot zombies but real ones. You wanna know if they're true. Just don't tell your mum – say to her it's a book about kids who eat their own bogies and she'll be too disgusted to ask any more questions.

Right, first of all this section of the book has no amnesia chips installed in the full-stops. You will remember this information; In fact you may need to remember this stuff.

Second, don't be freaked out. We don't need scaredy-cat freakery going on when the poop hits the propeller. We need you to be calm, controlled and in command.

Recently the Center of Disease Control in Atlanta, USA released an announcement stating. "CDC does not know of a virus or condition that would reanimate the dead (or one that would present zombie-like symptoms)"

What the blooming heck?!!!! That's the scientific equivalent of a football chairman passing a vote of confidence in the manager of a relegation threatened team. Two weeks later, they sack him. That means this stuff could actually happen!

*In the past, the CDC has published 'tongue-in-cheek'
zombie survival guides. These guys were trying to be funny
and clever and a little bit too smart for their own good. This
is a government agency, for goodness sake; they shouldn't
be messing around with the facts! This ruins the officialness
of anything else they do. Now they've been forced to put
out a statement saying 'Zombies Do Not Exist'.*

*So why have they been sending out 'Zombie Warnings'
like disaster-preparedness information. Just for a laugh? It's
coming true, I tell ye!*

*Several incidents, including a man arrested in Miami for
a horrific face-eating incident, see *1, have taken place
recently, as well as other examples of seemingly subhuman
behaviour, all around the same time, see *2-7. Many people
are now wondering what's behind this flesh-munching
wave of terror.*

*And my big fear now, whilst I'm writing this is…Will my
book be out soon enough to warn people? If you're reading
this safely at home, then there's still time.*

*But the public are confused, (and let's be honest, it's not
difficult to confuse Americans! Except if you are reading this
in America, then it's not difficult to confuse Canadians!)*

*Are zombies real or not? If they are just mythical monsters,
created by Hollywood to scare the bejeesus out of cinema-
goers, why is an official Government agency getting
involved? Methinks the lady doth protest too much, to
paraphrase Shakespeare's Hamlet.*

Let's look at the facts…

**1 In May 2012 in Miami, Florida, a mad guy attacked
a homeless man and was fired at by police while in the
process of biting the smelly tramp. The victim miraculously
survived and it is believed that the would-be zombie was
shot for refusing to stop eating his victim's butt. Source –
ABC News, MSN News, Daily Mail (Real news agencies and*

proper newspapers reported this stuff. I'm not making it up)

*2 Soon afterwards, a student in Maryland allegedly admitted to chopping up his roommate and then eating his heart and brain for his dinner Yuck! Source – ABC News, Daily Mail

*3 Around the same time, there was a "mysterious rash" breakout reported at a high school in Florida, which HazMat and disease control teams still cannae explain. Source – Huffington Post

*4 Two days later and HazMat crews were called in to Fort Lauderdale International Airport to determine the source of an "unknown chemical" that sent five people to the hospital. The exact cause is still not confirmed. Source - Gawker News

*5 Recently a doctor (yup, a blooming doctor) was arrested by the Florida Highway Patrol near Orlando and thrown into the back of the police car. He was so agitated and enraged he repeatedly banged his head on the patrol car's plexi-glass partition "until he bled." Source - Gawker News

*6 A few days later, a second outbreak of a mystery rash was reported at yet another Broward County school, Florida. A HazMat team was once again called in to investigate, and once again left without any concrete answers. Source - Gawker News

*7 The following day, a "disoriented" Canadian man was arrested onboard an American Airlines plane after he inexplicably attempted to rush the cockpit. The plane had just landed in Miami. Source - Gawker News

I hope you're no' reading on plane, heading towards Florida on your holidays.

There's something going on there.

Grandpa Jock's Guide to This Stuff Actually Happening

Here are five scientific reasons that I know madness like this will happen. And Dr Nobby thinks so too.

Drugs
Not the good stuff that the doctor gives you when you're ill. I mean natural chemicals, really evil, poisonous stuff from plants and flowers that mad witch doctors mix up and you have no idea where they came from. Mother Nature can grow stuff that can really mess us up so never take drugs, unless your mum says it's okay.

These neurotoxins slow your bodily functions down to the point that you'll be considered dead and you'll not even remember it. But, and this is mental bit, victims can be brought back to life, still under the effects of another drug, and leaves them roaming around, moaning and groaning and even doing simple tasks, like farming or even as a traffic warden.

Dr Nobby mentioned that this was what originally took place in Haiti a few years ago. It's really happened!

Virus
This is what the CDC was talking about when they said 'or one that would present zombie-like symptoms'.

Imagine a virus that turns humans into mindless killing machines. Kinda like cows that get Mad Dow Disease, we'd stagger around, stumbling and falling over, we'd see things that weren't there; we'd be twitching away and drooling all over ourselves.

When humans are infected with Mad Cow disease it's called Creutzfeldt-Jakob disease but fortunately the sufferers don't go around eating people. Yet.

However, our brains are only one little chemical away from messing up our whole world. If our brains stopped absorbing something called serotonin, we'd soon be a raging bunch of mentalists without the capability to know right from wrong and we'd be really, really aggressive too.

Watch out for those mad scientists!

Brain Parasites

This is Mother Nature messing with us again - Bugs that turn their victims into mindless zombie-like slaves. There's one cheeky chappy called Toxoplasmosa Gondii that devotes its entire existence to being super-bad and super-scary.

Mainly infecting rats, (It's worrying when the scientists say 'mainly') this weird disease can only breed inside the intestines of cats and the bug knows it needs to get the rat inside the cat. (I'm a freaky poet and I just don't know it!)

Then the parasite takes over the rat's brain, deliberately making the little rodent scurry towards a bunch of cats. The bug has actually programmed the rat to get itself eaten. It's like humans wanting to swim with sharks. Cages? Who needs 'em!

Neurogenisis

Not Mother Nature this time but those mad scientists again. Some of those nutters have been messing around with some weird stuff called stem cell research. Basically, they're just trying to re-generate dead cells and next they'll be re-growing dead brain tissue.

You see, scientists are already able to re-grow the brains of head trauma patients until they wake up and walk around again with mindless bodies and no personality. These nutters have even kept chickens walking around 18 months after they've been beheaded.

So it's only a matter of time before they do this with people. Bampots!

Nanobots

From bampots to nanobots. These tiny, little self-replicating robots can only be seen under a microscope and the industrious wee beasts can invisibly build or destroy anything, even inside the human body.

Those mental scientists have already created nano-cyborgs by mashing together a silicone chip and a virus and they can operate for up to a month after the death of the host. Basically, until your body starts to rot and your legs and arms fall off.

They cause zombification by crawling around inside the dead person's head, rewiring neural connections and replacing damaged ones and it would appear like that person is coming 'back to life'. They can create their own neural pathways, meaning they can use your brain to keep moving your arms and legs after you're dead.

But a month's not very long, so once these nanobots learn self-preservation, they'll jump to a new host by programming their zombie to bite someone and all the little robots will slide into the new body via the salvia, drool, snots or blood. Once inside they'll shut down the healthy brain cortex and take over.

Noo, I dinnae want to start a panic or nothing. This might no' happen for years. But it's better you start keeping your fingers crossed though...

However all is not lost. Follow my simple set of rules and you'll be fine.

(Courtesy of CDC)

How to survive a zombie apocalypse

- Don't panic. Panicking involves wetting your pants. It's harder to run in wet trousers.
- Get away from the zombies (D'uh). Most of the time, you can move faster than they can, they tend to zigzag and stagger all over the place (except if it's those freaky fast zombies).
- Gather food (not beans, you don't want to be trapped in a cellar where everyone is eating beans), water, an emergency radio, flashlights and weapons, and retreat to a secure location.
- If possible, retreat to a shopping mall, general retail store or other location where you'll have easy access to food and supplies. And stay there, Allison!
- Stay away from densely populated areas, where the infestation is likely to be heaviest ie school.
- Keep extra supplies of spare underwear. Pant pooping is to be expected.
- Remember that anyone sneezed on by a snot zombie (or bitten by the vicious ones) will become a threat to you and your party.
- Wait patiently for rescue and make long-term preparations for your survival.

Also, avoid common mistakes like:
- Sheltering in a vehicle to which you do not have the keys. Run, you fool!
- Leaving snotty hankies, blades or other basic weapons out for zombies to find.
- Teaching zombies how to use firearms. That would be stupid.
- Giving your only weapon to anyone who is hysterical. Even more stupider!

- Retreating to a basement or cellar without taking supplies with you. You'll get hungry.
- Getting into an elevator in a building infested with zombies. You'll get stuck.

And Finally, Another Science Bit.
I mentioned this earlier so just to prove I'm not making this stuff up...

*That newfound fungus in the Brazilian rain forest is called Ophiocordyceps camponoti-balzani. It infects the brain of ants and forces the diseased zombie ant to move to a good location for plant growth, then kills the insect. Source - Huffington Post

So, there you have it. The world is a bit mad, and will probably get madder. Zombies don't exist officially but we never expected the government to start a panic by saying they did. Of course they are going to deny it. Weird stuff happens and we're going to have to get used to it.

And there's not much weirder than an official government organisation putting out comics and creepy posters of zombies just to prepare people for some 'unknown' pandemic. I think they just might know something but they're not telling.

Unofficially zombies might exist if one or two mad scientists start messing around too much with stuff they shouldn't be messing with. Whether it's the dead coming back to life, or infected people rampaging around or even nanobot technology making people go loopy, George, Kenny, Allison and me have seen the future, except they can't remember any of it, and it's pant-poopingly scary.

And it's just as well George's memory was wiped because who wants to remember sucking the snot out of your head teacher's nose!

The End End

About the author, Stuart Reid

Stuart Reid is 48 years old, going on 10.

Throughout his early life he was dedicated to being immature, having fun and getting into trouble. After scoring a goal in the playground Stuart was known to celebrate by kissing lollypop ladies.

He is allergic to ties; blaming them for stifling the blood flow to his imagination throughout his twenties and thirties. After turning up at the wrong college, Stuart was forced to spend the next 25 years being boring, professional and corporate. His fun-loving attitude was further suppressed by the weight of career responsibility, as a business manager in the retail and hospitality industries in the UK and Dubai.

Stuart is one of the busiest authors in Britain, performing daily at schools, libraries, book stores and festivals with his book event Reading Rocks! He has appeared at over 950 schools and has performed to over 200,000 children. In 2015 Stuart was invited to tour overseas, with visits to schools in Ireland, Dubai and Abu Dhabi, performing for 120 princes at the Royal Rashid School For Boys.

He has performed his energetic and exciting book readings at the Edinburgh Fringe Festival, has been featured on national television, radio and countless newspapers and magazines. He won the Forward National Literature Silver Seal in 2012 for his debut novel, Gorgeous George and the Giant Geriatric Generator and was recently presented with the Enterprise in Education Champion Award by Falkirk Council.

Stuart has been married for over twenty years. He has two children, a superman outfit and a spiky haircut.

About the illustrator, John Pender

John is 37 and currently lives in Grangemouth with his wife Angela and their young son, Lucas, aged 6.

Working from his offices in Glasgow, John has been a professional graphic designer and illustrator since he was 18 years old, contracted to create illustrations, artwork and digital logos for businesses around the world, along with a host of individual commissions of varying degrees.

Being a comic book lover since the age of 4, illustration is his true passion, doodling everything from the likes of Transformers, to Danger Mouse to Spider-man and Batman in pursuit of honing his skills over the years.

As well as cartoon and comic book art, John is also an accomplished digital artist, specialising in a more realistic form of art for this medium, and draws his inspiration from acclaimed names such as Charlie Adlard, famous for The Walking Dead graphic novels, Glenn Fabry from the Preacher series, as well as the renowned Dan Luvisi, Leinil Yu, Steve McNiven and Gary Frank.

John has been married to Angela for 7 years and he describes his wife as his 'source of inspiration, positivity and motivation for life.' John enjoys the relaxation and stress-relief that family life can bring.

Photography is another of John's pleasures, and has established a loyal and enthusiastic following on Instagram.

The Gorgeous George Books

Gorgeous George and the Giant Geriatric Generator
The first Gorgeous George Adventure
Bogies, baddies, bagpipes and burps!
Farting, false teeth and fun!
Kindle: http://goo.gl/tXB7x4

Gorgeous George and the ZigZag Zit-faced Zombies

Sneezing, sniffing, snogging and snots. Zombies, zebras and zits!

**Gorgeous George and the Unidentified
Unsinkable Underpants Part 1**

Poo, plesiosaurs, porridge, pants! Monsters, mayhem & muck!

**Gorgeous George and the Unidentified
Unsinkable Underpants Part 2**

More monsters, more mayhem and more muck.
And pot-loads of porridge, poo, pumps and pants!

Gorgeous George and the Jumbo Jobby Juicer

Burgers, bottoms, baddies and burps.
Power pink, pumping and poop!

www.stuart-reid.com